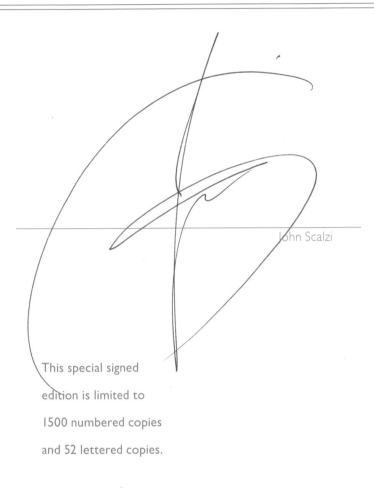

John Scalzi

This special signed
edition is limited to
1500 numbered copies
and 52 lettered copies.

This is copy **913**.

MINIATURES:

The Very Short Fiction of John Scalzi

MINIATURES:

The Very Short Fiction of John Scalzi

By

John Scalzi

SUBTERRANEAN PRESS 2016

First Edition

ISBN
978-1-59606-812-4

See pages 141-142 for individual story credits.

Subterranean Press
PO Box 190106
Burton, MI 48519

subterraneanpress.com

Dedication

To everyone who I made read my fiction in high school.
Sorry, folks. I got better at it.
No, really.

CONTENTS:

Introduction, or,
Let's Keep This Short

I've often thought that as a fiction writer I have two natural speeds: Novel length—over 40,000 words, and usually closer to 100,000 words—and *really* short, as in about 2,000 words or less.

It's not that I can't write at other lengths; in my professional fiction life I've written short stories, novelettes and novellas, enjoyed them, and have done just fine with them. What I'm saying is that the easiest lengths for me, and the ones that I enjoy the most in terms of the act of writing, are the longest and the very shortest.

The novels are not here in this collection (I mean, *duh*). But a lot of the very shortest are.

In terms of the very shortest lengths, I think my ease and enjoyment of them comes from two separate sources: Journalism and humor. Before I started writing fiction I worked for a newspaper, where I was a film critic and opinion columnist. In both cases, you didn't have a whole lot of space to make your point—a column was usually eight hundred words, and reviews were often shorter than that. If you got a thousand words to write something, that was a luxury.

Fast, punchy and to the point: That was the goal. I wrote thousands of reviews and dozens of columns as a newspaperman, and got used writing short.

As for the other source, humor: Well. If drama is a marathon, humor is a sprint. Get in, make 'em laugh, get out.

There are 18 pieces in the collection, the longest of which is a whopping 2,296 words long, including the title; the shortest, just 427 words. The average piece length is 1,310 words. The forms of the stories— interviews, memos, even Twitter posts and search results—have brevity in mind. Nearly all of them are meant to be funny (one's not. You'll know it when you see it).

Four of the pieces are original to this collection; they've never been printed elsewhere. Other pieces have been in the archives long enough that this is probably the first time most humans will see them. The writing dates for the pieces here range from 1991 to literally this very afternoon. One of these pieces was nominated for an award. And one of them is a poem. Finally, I'll be a published poet! This will annoy real poets, I'm sure. Sorry, real poets.

In any event: These pieces are meant to be short and sweet. Hope you enjoy them all. But if there's one you don't like, don't worry. It'll be over soon.

—John Scalzi
April 17, 2016

This is my first professionally published science fiction story, which showed up in the Strange Horizons *online magazine in October of 2001. It's also the very first science fiction story I ever wrote as an adult; all the ones before this one were written in high school and I never submitted them anywhere.* Strange Horizons *was the first place it was submitted to (because I liked the magazine and also, they took online submissions), so it was a nice confidence boost to sell something right out of the gate.*

Alien Animal Encounters

By John Scalzi, Staff Writer, *Sol System Weekly Report*

Each week, we here at *SSWR* step right outside of our offices here on 54th and ask folks on the street our Question of the Week—sometimes topical, sometimes whimsical, always intriguing. Our question this week:

What is the most interesting encounter you've ever had with an alien animal species?

Rowenna Morello, Accountant, Staten Island:

That's gotta be the time we got the cat high with a glyph. My college roommate worked in the xenobiology lab and brought the glyph home one night in a shoebox. It's just this little mouse-like thing, so of course the cat wanted at it right away. It's cat-food-sized. We pushed the cat away from it a couple of times, but then I had to go make a call. I left the glyph alone in its box on the table, and the cat hopped up and started poking at the thing with its paw, you know, poke poke poke.

Thing is, the glyph is a total predator, and it's got this mouth that opens up like a little umbrella and surrounds whatever it's going to eat. So there's the cat, batting at the glyph, and suddenly the glyph lunges forward, opens its jaws, wraps them around the cat's paw, and clamps down hard. It's trying to eat the cat. Well, the cat's freaking out, of course. It's scooting backwards, trying frantically to shake this thing off its paw and wailing, you know, like a cat in heat. My roommate had to use a Popsicle stick from the trash to pry the glyph's mouth open.

The cat ran away and seemed to be pissed off but okay. Then a half hour later I caught him just staring at a bookshelf and wobbling back and forth. Seems that glyphs paralyze their prey with venom; it kills just about anything on the glyphs' planet but here it just makes you hallucinate. It's a chemistry thing. After we realized the cat wasn't going to die, it was actually pretty funny to watch him bump into walls and stare at his own paws. Although at one point he sprinted right towards an open window and my roommate had to make a lunge to keep him from jumping out. It was a third-floor walkup. I guess the cat thought he could fly.

Anyway, the glyph went back to the lab the next day. The funny thing is that for the next couple of days, the cat seemed to be looking around to find the glyph, circling the table and poking into boxes and stuff. I think he wanted a fix.

Alan Jones-Wynn, Copywriter, Manhattan:

My daughter's third-grade class was taking a trip to the Bronx Zoo and it was my turn to be a parent assistant, so I got the day off from work and helped her teacher herd a couple dozen kids around the place, which, if you've never done it, is just as aggravating as it sounds. This was around the time that the zoo was just opening their "Alien Animals" exhibit, and the place was jam-packed; it actually helped that we were on an official educational field trip, because otherwise we probably wouldn't have been able to get through the crowds.

We filed through and the tour guide pointed out all the popular alien animals, like those omads and the revers and the neyons, right, the ones they make stuffed-animal toys of to sell at the gift shop. But then we came to this one habitat and the tour guide stopped and pointed out what had to have been the ugliest lump of fur in the whole zoo. She told us that the lump we were looking at was called a corou, and that it was an endangered species on Tungsk, and that the Bronx Zoo and others were trying to start a captive breeding program. As she was saying this, her eyes were welling up with tears, and it seemed like she was about to break down right then and there.

Well, obviously, this seemed like pretty bizarre behavior, but then I looked at the corou, and it swiveled an eye stalk at me, and I swear I was overwhelmed with this wave of sadness and regret that was so overpowering I can't even describe it. It's like what you'd probably feel if you'd just heard that a bus carrying everyone you ever knew just went off a mountain trail in Peru. And it wasn't just me; all those kids, who you couldn't have shut up if you wired their jaws shut, were all just standing there silently, staring at the corou and looking like they'd just seen their dog run over by a car. One of the kids actually tapped on the glass of the habitat and said "I'm sorry" to the corou, over and over. We had to literally drag some of the kids away. I mean, I wouldn't call it telepathy or mind control, but something was going on there.

My kid and I went back a couple of years later and the corou exhibit wasn't there anymore, and I was sort of glad—it's never a good thing to worry that you're going to get clinically depressed at the zoo. At a dinner party a little later I met a vet who worked at the zoo, and I asked him about the corou. He said that one zoologist working with the habitat committed suicide and another was placed on leave after she took the zoo's breeding pair, drove them up to Vermont, and tried to release them into the wild. She kept telling everyone afterwards that they told her it was what they wanted. They eventually had to get rid of the exhibit altogether. I haven't heard about the corou since. I think they're extinct now.

Ted McPeak, Community College Student, Jersey City:

Some friends and me heard that if you smoked the skin of an aret, you could get monumentally wasted. So we bought one at a pet store and waited a couple of weeks until it shed its skin. Then we crumbled up the dry skin, put it in with some pot, and lit up. We all got these insane mouth blisters that didn't go away for weeks. We all had to eat soup for a month. Though maybe it wasn't the skin; the pot could have been bad or something. We flushed the aret down the toilet after we got the blisters, though, so we'd have to go buy a new one to try it out again. I don't think we'll bother.

Qa' Hungran Ongru, Cultural Attaché for Fine Arts and Literature, Royal Kindran Embassy, Manhattan:

Well, I am myself an alien here, so I suppose you could say that my most interesting incident with an alien animal was with one of your animals, a dog. Shortly after being assigned to the embassy here, I was given a Shih Tzu by a human friend. I was delighted, of course. He really was an adorable thing, and he was very loving and devoted to me. I named him Fred. I like that name.

As you may know, the male of the Kindra species is a large non-sentient segmented worm which we females attach across our midriffs during the mating process; the male stays attached while a four-part fertilization process occurs over several days. It's not very romantic by human standards, but obviously it works well for us. Shortly before one of my ovulatory periods, I had managed to score a rather significant diplomatic coup when I convinced the Guggenheim to tour selections of its collection among the Kindra home planets. As a reward I was allowed to choose a male from the oligarchical breeding stock for my next insemination. The one I chose had deep segment ridges and a nicely mottled scale pattern; again, not something a human would find attractive, but deeply compelling for Kindrae. He was attached to me in a brief conjoining ceremony at the embassy, attended by selected Kindra and human friends, and then I went home to Fred.

Fred came running to meet me at the door as he always did, but when he saw the male across my belly, he skidded across the tiles and then started growling and barking and backing away slowly. I tried to assure him that everything was okay, but every time I tried to reach for Fred, he'd back away more. At one point he snapped at my tendrils. I was surprisingly hurt; although it seemed silly to want Fred and the male to "get along" (considering that the male was doing nothing but lying there), I did want them to get along. If for no other reason than that the male would be attached to me for the next week or so. But for the next few days Fred would have nothing to do with me. He wouldn't eat from his bowl until I left the room. He even peed in my shoes.

On the fourth night of this, I was sleeping when I suddenly felt a sharp pain in my abdomen; it was the male, beginning to unhook himself from me. Then I heard the growling. I snapped on a light, looked down, and saw Fred attacking the male; he had managed to get a bite in between two of the male's ring segments and punctured an artery. The male was bleeding all over my bed. If the male managed to completely detach himself, it would be disastrous—my impregnation cycle was not yet complete, and it would be highly unlikely after a noble male was attacked in my bed that I would be entrusted with another ever again. So with one arm I lodged the male back onto me and struggled to keep him in place, with another I reached for the phone to call my doctor, and with the third I scooped up Fred and tossed him off the bed. He landed up on the floor with a yelp and limped away, winding up a perfectly charming incident for all three of us.

I was rushed to the embassy infirmary, where the male's injuries were sutured and he was sedated to the point where he would again willingly reattach himself to me. By some miracle the fertilization process was uninterrupted; I was confined to an infirmary bed for the rest of the process while doctors made sure everything went as it was supposed to. The ambassador came to visit afterwards and I expressed my shame at the incident and offered my resignation; she declined it, and told me that no one blamed me for what happened, but that it would probably be a good idea to get rid of Fred.

I did, giving him to a retired human diplomat I had worked with for many years. I visit them both frequently, and Fred is always happy to see me. He's also always happy to see my daughter. Who is also named Fred. As I said, I like the name.

Dr. Elliot Morgenthal, Doctor, Stamford:
Oh, God. I worked the ER as an intern right around the time of that stupid fungdu craze. Here's

the thing about fungdu: they're furry, they're friendly, they vibrate when they're happy, and they have unusually large toothless mouths. You can see where this is going. About two or three times a month we'd get some poor bastard coming in with a fungdu on his Johnson.

What people apparently don't know about fungdu is that if they think that what they've got in their mouths is live prey, these little backward-pointing quills emerge out of their gums to keep whatever they're trying to eat from escaping. These dumbasses get it into their heads to get a hummer from their fungdu, and then are understandably surprised to discover that their pet thinks it's being fed a live hot dog. Out come the quills, and the next thing you know, there's some asshole in the emergency room trying to explain how his erect penis just happened to fall into the fungdu's mouth. He tripped, you see. How inconvenient.

Here's the truly disgusting thing about this: All the time this is going on, the fungdu is usually desperately trying to swallow. And that animal has some truly amazing peristaltic motion. Again, you can see where this is going. The nurses wouldn't touch any of these guys. They told them to clean up after their own damn selves. Who can blame them.

Bill and Sue Dukes, Plumbing Supplies, Queens:

Bill: There was this one time I was driving through Texas, and I saw the weirdest fuckin' thing on the side of the road. It looked like an armor-plated rabbit or something. It was just lying there, though. I think it was dead.

Sue: You idiot. That's an armadillo. They're from Earth.

Bill: No, you must be thinking of some other animal. This thing was totally not Earth-like at all. It had, like, scales and shit.

Sue: That's an armadillo. They're all over Texas. They're like the state animal or something. Everybody knows that.

Bill: Well, what the fuck do I know about Texas? I'm from Queens. And we sure as hell don't got any armadillos in Queens.

Sue (rolling eyes): Oh, yeah, if it's not from Queens, it ain't shit, right?

Bill: You got that right. Fuckin' Texas. Hey, what about those things, you know, that got the duck bill?

Sue: You mean ducks?

Bill: No, smartass, they don't look like a duck, they just got a duck bill.

Sue: What, a platypus?

Bill: Yeah, a platypus! Where are those things from?

Sue: They're from Earth too.

Bill: No shit? Man, Earth is a weird-ass planet sometimes.

Missives from Possible Futures #1: Alternate History Search Results

Dear Customer,

Thank you for trying a Sample History Search with Multiversity™, America's leading Alternate History Research Firm. Thanks to our patented Multiview™ technology, and search algorithms that scour multiple universes with more speed and accuracy, Multiversity™ is able to access nearly 50% more alternate timestreams than either Alternaview or Megapast—for the same cost! And we guarantee our alternate history research with a 100% money back guarantee—we want you to be happy with the accuracy of our alternate pasts, so we can work together in our shared future.

For your Sample History Search, you asked to see THE DEATH OF ADOLF HITLER on the date of AUGUST 13, 1908 in VIENNA, AUSTRIA. As it happens, THE DEATH OF ADOLF HITLER is one of our most popular requests, and Multiversity™ has developed an impressive pre-cached concordance on the subject, spanning most days of this subject's entire lifespan. What does this mean for you? Simply that as a pre-researched event, if you were paying for this History Search, we could offer you this information on a substantially discounted basis: Some popular searches are available for as much as 65% off the "new search" price!

As you did not specify the particular details for THE DEATH OF ADOLF HITLER on AUGUST 13, 1908 in VIENNA, AUSTRIA, we are proud to offer you a random sampler of scenarios relating to the disposition of your search. In it you will see how varying the details of the event you've chosen can greatly influence the course of history. This is the famous "Butterfly Effect"—and we're sure you'll enjoy seeing the storms these butterflies bring about!

Because this is a Sample History Search, we regret that we may only provide summaries at this time. But should you wish to explore one or more of these alternate histories in greater detail, Multiversity™ is proud to offer you a Detailed Historical Statement—a $300 value—for just $59.95. Please contact one of our sales representatives to take advantage of this Special Offer!

Thanks again for choosing Multiversity™—It's a great time to be with us™.

Scenario #1

Event: ADOLF HITLER is KILLED by MUGGING ATTEMPT ON THE STEPS OF THE ACADEMY OF FINE ARTS VIENNA

As a result: World War I proceeds; Weimar Republic proceeds; World War II delayed until 1948; US drops atomic bomb on Berlin in 1952; Neil Armstrong first man on the moon, 1972

Scenario #2

Event: ADOLF HITLER is KILLED by OPIUM JUNKIE LOOKING FOR MONEY

As a result: World War I proceeds; Weimar Republic proceeds; World War II averted; Germany and Britain form economic union, declare war on France in 1958; Malcolm Evans first man on the moon, 1975

Scenario #3:

Event: ADOLF HITLER is KILLED by RUN-AWAY HORSE-DRAWN WAGON FILLED WITH BRATWURST, THE FOURTH SUCH FATALITY IN VIENNA IN SIX DAYS

As a result: Vienna passes tough horse-drawn vehicle laws, prompting the quick acceptance of automobiles; Austria becomes automotive industrial powerhouse; World War I proceeds, Germany and allies win thanks to technological advances; 30s worldwide depression averted; Willy Brandt first man on the moon, 1958

Scenario #4:

Event: ADOLF HITLER is KILLED by MULTIPLE KNIFE WOUNDS BY JEALOUS GAY LOVER WHO

THINKS HIS BOYFRIEND IS CHEATING ON HIM WITH HITLER, WHO IN FACT IS TOTALLY IN-NOCENT AND HASN'T HAD SEX OF ANY SORT IN MONTHS, MUCH LESS GAY VIENNESE SEX

As a result: The trial of Felix von Weingartner, director of the Vienna Opera and the closeted, mur-dering gay lover in question, shocks and delights Viennese society; Hitler's watercolors, formerly unsell-able, become a hot commodity on the auction circuit before the novelty wears off. Hitler's sister awarded a settlement; World War I proceeds, Germany and allies win; 30s depression not averted; virulent flu wipes out 38% of European population; US becomes world power; John Glenn first man on the moon, 1956

Scenario #5

Event: ADOLF HITLER is KILLED by SUFFO-CATION WHEN INEXPLICABLY ENCASED IN AN ENORMOUS BLOCK OF UNFLAVORED GELATIN

As a result: Hitler only a random test subject for Gelatin Encasing Weapon, developed by the Russian aristocracy from technology pulled out of the space-ship that caused the Tunguska Event of June 30, 1908; the GEW subsequently used to assassinate enemies of Tsar Nicholas II, and then world leaders; World War I begins when Archduke Franz Ferdinand is spon-taneously encased in gelatin while riding in a 1911 Graf und Stift Rois De Blougne tourer in Sarajevo and Young Bosnia opportunistically claims credit; World War I subsequently ends in 1915 when entire German divisions are gelatinized; Russia becomes sole super power; Vladimir Putin first man on the moon, 1988

Scenario #6

Event: ADOLF HITLER is KILLED by BULLET WOUND IN CROSSFIRE BETWEEN TIME-TRAVELING ANTI-NAZIS SENT BACK TO KILL HIM AND TIME-TRAVELING NAZIS SENT BACK TO PREVENT HIS ASSASSINATION

As a result: Causality loop annihilates time and space surrounding Vienna, knocking everyone in the city back to 1529 and the eve of the First Turkish Seige; as the 20th century Viennese use their historical knowledge to help the 16th Century Viennese, time-traveling pro-Viennese forces appear and fight a pitched battle with time-traveling pro-Ottoman forces, pushing everyone back to 955 and the Battle of Lechfeld; when the time-traveling pro-Magyar forces show up, they are slaughtered by everyone else which is tired of all this time-traveling crap, thereby ending the causality loop. Vienna becomes world power; Henry Jasomirgott first man on the moon, 1155

Scenario #7

Event: ADOLF HITLER is KILLED by MARATHON FORNICATION BY SIX VIENNESE PROSTITUTES

As a result: Prostitutes arrested and revealed as libidinous time-travelers from a very sexy future who teach the Viennese their futuristic ways of astro-pleasure; Janine Lindemulder first woman on the moon, 1996

Scenario #8

Event: ADOLF HITLER is KILLED by VAPORIZATION WHEN METEOR HITS HIM SQUARE ON THE HEAD

As a result: No noticeable historical changes arise from event at all. However, as the meteor is a precursor to a massive asteroid cruising toward Earth, human history had only 22 hours, 16 minutes to develop from that point before being obliterated. Humanity wiped out along with Hitler and 93% of all species; society of rats rises and falls; society of frogs rises and falls; society of pillbugs rises and falls; society of squid rises and sticks; Gluugsnertgluug first squid on the moon, 2,973,004,412

Written after the de-planetization of Pluto in 2006. I'm still bitter about it.

Pluto Tells All

By Pluto, ex-planet, 4,500,000,000 years old

As told to John Scalzi

I don't want to sound like I was surprised, but yeah, I was surprised. Because just before, they were talking about adding planets, right? Me and Eris and possibly Ceres, and it looked like that proposal was getting good play. So it looked good, and Charon and I thought it'd be okay to take a break and get a little alone time. So there we are relaxing and then suddenly my agent Danny's on the phone, telling me about the demotion. And I say to him, I thought you had this taken care of. That's what you told me. And he said, well, they took another vote. And then he started trying to spin the demotion like it was a positive. Look at Phil Collins, he said. He was an ex-member of Genesis but then he had this huge solo career. And I said, first, Phil Collins *sucks*, and second, I'm not exactly the lead singer of the solar system, am I? This isn't the Phil Collins scenario, it's the Pete Best scenario. I'm the Pete Best of the goddamn solar system. So I fired Danny. Now I'm with CAA.

No, really. Phil Collins does suck. I'm sorry, but there it is. Good drummer, but a lot of his sound is from his producer, Hugh Padgham. You want to sound like Phil Collins? Have your producer drop in a noise gate. Done. And his *singing*. Oy. Funny thing is, in the 80s, Phil was in talks to play me in a science fiction comedy. He dropped out of it and made *Buster* instead. The movie deal fell apart after that. I lost some money on that. I have some issues with Phil Collins.

The funny thing about the demotion is that I never actually wanted to be a planet, you know? I was out here minding my own business and then suddenly Clyde Tombaugh is staring at me. And the next thing I know, people start calling me and telling me I'm the newest planet. And I remember saying, I don't know if I want that responsibility. And they said, well, you can't not be a planet *now*, Walt Disney's already named a character after you. That's really what made me a planet. Not the astronomers, but that cartoon dog. People loved that dog.

Ironically, I'm a cat person.

I'm not going to sue. Who am I going to sue? You think the International Astronomical Union has any money to speak of? There's a reason the most popular event at an astronomer's conference is the free buffet.

I try to look at it philosophically. Seventy-six years is a fine run. And now I'm sort of the spokesperson for an entirely new class of objects: The dwarf planets. I understand it's meant to be something of a consolation prize, but you know what, there are more of us dwarf planets out here than anything else. If we're talking "one dwarf planet, one vote," you're going to find we're setting the agenda on a lot of things.

I might make a comeback. There are some groups rebelling against the new definition right now. And there are a lot of people telling me they want to work with me. It's not *just* NASA anymore. Let's just say CAA is earning its fee.

Yes, I'm excited about the New Horizons mission. But I wish you guys could have found a way to get one of the Voyagers my way. I wanted to listen to that record.

I think most people know I had no direct involvement in *The Adventures of Pluto Nash.* That movie took place on *your* moon, folks.

"Dwarf planet" is a misnomer. If I sit in your lap, you're gonna feel me.

"Plutoed"? Has anyone ever actually used that word? Even I don't use it, and it *happened* to me. I think it's some sort of urban myth.

The worst thing about it all is that Eris feels like it's her fault, like if she'd never been discovered then they wouldn't have had an excuse to kick me out. She's a sweet kid. She shouldn't have to feel like it has anything to do with her.

Yes, it's cold this far out from the sun. But look, I'm mostly made of ice. I get any closer, I'd get melty, and then suddenly I'm the size of Vesta. Then I really *will* be a dwarf planet.

No, no. Some of my best friends are asteroids.

I'll tell you when I think the problem started. A few years ago the director of the Rose Center for Earth and Space asked for a favor. A big fat unethical favor. I said to him that I was too big to fit in a jail cell but he was just the right size, and I didn't want that for him. He got snippy, I got snippy back, but I thought that was that—it's business. A little while later they do that panorama of the solar system of theirs, and I've been dropped from it, and the Rose Center spokesman is saying I'm the "King of the Trans-Neptunian Objects" in that patronizing way of his. I should have done the director his favor and let him rot when he got caught.

It's not what you think. Just because I'm named for the god of the underworld, it doesn't mean I have *connections.*

I have problems with the new definition, yeah. What is this "sweep your lane" shit? Let me toss Eris at your planet and see what sort of job Earth does sweeping the lane. I don't think you'd like the result. Look, when people want you gone, they'll use any excuse. Simple as that.

Also, highly elliptical orbits are *fun.* You don't know what you're missing, people.

One thing about something like this is you find out who your friends are. Jupiter couldn't have been nicer during the whole thing. Saturn's been a real sweetheart, too. And Neptune—well, we go way back. We're simpatico, always have been. But some others, eh. Not so nice.

No, I don't want to name names. They know who they are.

Oh, fine. Mercury. I got into the club, and Mercury was suddenly my best buddy. And I thought, well, okay—we're close to the same size, both of us have eccentric orbits, we've both got a 3:2 resonance thing going on. Similarities, you know? So we hang out, get to know each other, fine, whatever. Then the IAU vote comes down and I haven't heard from him since. Like the demotion might be catching or something. He may be right; he's not exactly a brilliant lane-sweeper himself.

Evidence? Well, you know. It's not that he has an unusually thick iron core; it's that he's got an unusually thin silicate skin. Where did the rest of it go? So much for lane-sweeping. See, now you know why he's so damn twitchy. A perfect example of small planet syndrome.

No, I don't have small planet syndrome. I have dwarf planet syndrome. Didn't you get the memo?

You know who else have been nice? Moons. If anyone had reason to be bitter about me being made a planet, it was them. Hell, you can't tell me Titan doesn't deserve to be a planet: He's got an atmosphere, for God's sake. Not one of them ever said anything against me. The day I got demoted, Titan calls up, says "you wuz robbed" and then tells me dirty jokes until I nearly throw up laughing. We should swap him for Mercury.

I have nothing bad to say about Earth. Good planet. Friendly. Too bad you people are making her all itchy recently. If I were her I would be considering a topical application of a meteor right about now. You're lucky she's tolerant.

One of the good things about the whole fracas was once it was settled, Eris finally got a permanent name. Being called "Xena" really ticked her off. She said that when Uranus was discovered, his temporary name was "Georgium Sidus," after King George III of England. He got a national leader, she got a butch TV character. I told her I didn't really think she wanted to be named "Dubya," and she said I had a point. Then I said her moon would have been named "Cheney," and then she hit me.

It hurts when you're hit by a dwarf planet. She's bigger than me, you know.

I would have preferred the term "ice planet" myself. Some of the "dwarf" planets out here are going to mess with that definition once you discover them.

No, I won't tell you where they are. Find them yourself. You guys are good at that.

Life on other planets? You know, I'm paid really well not to comment about that.

I will say that if there is life on other planets, that they'd wish you'd stop beaming "lite hits" music stations into space. I'm not the only one out here who has Phil Collins issues. Theoretically.

Denise Jones, Superbooker

(TRANSCRIPT BEGINS)

Q: Please state your name and your occupation.

A: My name is Denise Jones, and I'm the Super Hero Booking Coordinator for the International Society of Super Beings, formerly the National League of Super Beings, formerly The Liberty Friends.

Q: First off: Do you yourself have any super powers?

A: Not unless booking counts as a super power, no. I got the job through Craigslist.

Q: What does a booking coordinator do, in the context of super beings?

A: Well, as you know, cities and countries all over the world are under constant threat from terrorists, organized crime, natural disasters, arch villains and monsters both alien and supernatural. When these cities and countries find themselves under attack, they'll give me a call and I'll find them a super being affiliated with the ISSB to help them deal with whatever crisis they're dealing with at the moment.

Q: So you're saying that if Chicago were attacked by a sewer monster or something, the mayor would have to go through you to get help from ArachnoLad.

A: No, Chicago keeps ArachnoLad on a retainer. The Evening Stalker, too. Most large cities have one or two super beings under contract.

Q: So, Chicago pays ArachnoLad for protection?

A: You make it sound like a mob racket. It's more like a consulting and services fee. In exchange for certain considerations, Chicago can expect ArachnoLad to be a first responder to any arch villain or monster attack, with a certain number of contractually-agreed-to nights and evenings in which ArachnoLad freelances against common thugs and criminals, for deterrence purposes.

Q: When you say "certain considerations," you're talking about money.

A: Sure.

Q: That kind of goes against the idea of super beings doing this sort of thing out of the goodness of their hearts.

A: Well, do you work for free?

Q: No, but I'm not a super being.

A: Even super beings have to eat.

Q: I thought that was what secret identities were for. So they could have bill-paying day jobs.

A: Super beings haven't had day jobs since pagers and Blackberrys hit the market. There's no way you can get away from work anymore. And when Chicago is being attacked by a sewer monster, it doesn't want to have to wait for ArachnoLad to find some clever way to sneak out of a sales meeting. That's just stupid.

Q: Okay. Chicago and ArachnoLad notwithstanding, walk us through how someone gets a super being out of you.

A: All right. As I said before, most of the major cities in the US have a super being or two on retainer. So the calls I get are usually from mid-sized cities.

Q: Like, what, Oklahoma City?

A: Oklahoma City actually just put The Invisible Avenger under retainer.

Q: I thought he was in Seattle.

A: He was. Oklahoma offered him better terms. You know how it is. City gets ambitious. So not Oklahoma City. Let's say Fresno.

Q: Fresno it is.

A: Fresno has no in-house super being, so when disaster strikes, they give me a call. We look at the nature of their issue, who among the ISSB roster is available and appropriate, and then work to find someone who can respond on an expedited basis.

Q: So, let's say that Fresno is being attacked by a monster.

A: What kind of monster?

Q: A big one.

A: That's not specific enough. Is it an alien monster? Is it some sort of mutated animal? Is it shooting laser beams out of its eyes or does it have fire breath? Can it fly? Is it actually a massive colony of smaller creatures that form together and combine intelligences? All of this matters, you know.

Q: Yeah, but if the city is under attack, I don't think you'd have time to stop the monster and ask it what its weaknesses are.

A: Of course not. That's why we have the standard questionnaire.

Q: The monster's attacking and you're giving a questionnaire?

A: It's not that long. And by that point city officials are motivated to respond quickly.

Q: Okay. It's a Gila Lizard large enough to stomp a car, that shoots poison from its tear ducts.

A: Good. That's a Class Four monster, which is our classification for non-sentient mutated animal species, with the poison-casting sub-classification. Now, if this were a real emergency I would check the ISSB database, but off the top of my head I can tell you that there are three ISSB-affiliated super beings that could respond in under an hour with powers that would be useful for this particular mission: Battling Tiger in Glendale, ElectroBot in Emeryville and Bryan Garcia in San Jose.

Q: Bryan Garcia?

A: Yes. What about him?

Q: It's just not the usual sort of super being name.

A: He's new and he thinks the super being masked identities thing is kind of silly. He fights in jeans and t-shirt. Whatever makes him happy.

Q: I admire someone comfortable with their own identity, so let's say I pick him.

A: Then from there what we do is check his availability, agree on a consulting fee, and fax over waivers to be signed by the appropriate local authorities.

Q: What kind of waivers?

A: Indemnity for property damage, mostly.

Q: Right, because that usually happens.

A: It depends. Super villains are generally respectful of property, contrary to popular belief, because they usually have some economic goal in mind, and it's hard to put a city to work if you've blown up all the buildings with lasers. But Class Four monsters? Big time. They claw through skyscrapers looking for people to snack on. A super being shouldn't be on the hook for that.

Q: Cities won't really try to collect from the super being that saved their bacon, would they?

A: Are you kidding? The owners of the destroyed properties try to collect on their insurance, the insurance companies try to sue the city for negligence, and the city tries to pass the buck onto the super being. Happened in Tempe in 1993. The Crimson Valkyrie defeated the Gelatinous Menace and then lost everything she had. Had to quit. She works in a Jersey tollbooth now.

Q: That's awful.

A: It's awful for Tempe. Their calls don't get returned around here. They've been swallowed by the Gelatinous Menace six times since then. It's hell on property values. But the good news is other cities saw Tempe covered in goo and decided that trying to roll the blame for the damage onto the super being just wasn't the way go.

Q: Fair enough. Although if they're totally indemnified, super beings don't have any motivation not to level a city to get at the monster.

A: Sure they do. Most of the city contracts offer bonuses to the super being if the overall property damage is below, say, $10 million. The exact figure varies from case to case. But that's the amount on the standard contract.

Q: There's a standard contract?

A: Sure. When a monster is devouring your citizens like Pez, you want don't want to haggle too long.

Q: I guess not.

A: I mean, this is sort of why super beings join ISSB in the first place. Freelance monster fighting seems appealing at first blush, especially for those super beings who are moody and have problems working in a team setting. But if you show up somewhere and just start cracking skulls, your legal liability goes right through the roof. Seriously, you know what the difference between a super being and super villain is?

Q: Henchmen?

A: Contractual indemnification. Really, in a lot of cases that's just it. The Sinister Glove started out as a super being, you know. Then he started getting charged for damages and had to turn to crime to claw his way out of the debt hole. It's sad, really. He should have joined the ISSB at the beginning. But he didn't want to pay our finder's fee for each mission. Penny wise and pound foolish.

Q: But the Sinister Glove is now the uncontested master of Andorra, where he rules with an iron fist.

A: Iron glove.

Q: Right.

A: And that's an object lesson in what happens when a city or in this case a principality tries to cut corners in making a deal with the ISSB. When the Sinister Glove attacked with his army of hyperintelligent cyborg cats, we offered Andorra a really nice package of three super beings plus Sparkles the Robot Dog and his Running Pack, and an optional assist from Extraordinary Man if required—which isn't something we ever do, he's booked years in advance—and they tried to haggle. Wanted to pay in an installment plan. And in Euros. We can't take Euros. It's part of our tax deal with the US. By the time they were ready to get serious, the cyborg cats had already consumed the Prime Minister and two thirds of the legislature. And of course, by then it's too late.

Q: Well, you could have just had Extraordinary Man circle the globe backwards and turn back time, and then try again.

A: We did. Twice. Same result both times. After a certain point there's no percentage in trying anymore. And now look at Andorra.

Q: The world's smallest villainocracy.

A: Cyborg cats everywhere.

Q: Okay, so you help connect super beings to the places that need their services. But what about the downtime? I know the ISSB has something like 400 members in the US alone, but typically there's only a single arch villain or alien monster attack in the US a day. Even if you double up some of those contracts, we're still looking at 99.5% unemployment on a day-to-day basis.

A: That's right. So in addition to connecting super beings with cities in need, I also act as a conventional booker and schedule our members for corporate and public events.

Q: So, like, what, exactly?

A: Motivational speaking gigs are very popular. Encouraging people to live up to their potential, that sort of thing.

Q: No one seems to mind the irony of someone with super powers lecturing ordinary people on reaching their potential?

A: What do you mean?

Q: I'm just thinking of those corporate events where they have people walk on coals as a way to show they can do anything. For a super being, that's not exactly a great feat.

A: It depends on the super being, really. LubricantGrrl wouldn't like that particular event.

Q: There's a super being named LubricantGrrl?

A: She saved Reno last month from the Sandpaper People.

Q: I missed that one.

A: She got them before they reached the casinos. Not much of a write-up. But yes, she's one of our more specialized members.

Q: I bet she'd be popular at parties.

A: In fact we do book private parties, although, let me be clear, not the sort you just implied, for which I'm offended on behalf of LubricantGrrl.

Q: Sorry. What kind of parties?

A: Birthdays, weddings, bar mitzvahs.

Q: Instead of, say, a clown.

A: I wouldn't put it that way. There's a certain segment of society that enjoys celebrity appearances at their events. We've all heard stories of how some people will get Coldplay or Hannah Montana to play their kid's birthday party. Same concept, different skill set.

Q: Are there indemnity riders in those contracts too?

A: You bet there are. You would not believe how many kids want to go flying with a super being, and then eat a bug at 5,000 feet and go screaming to mommy, who then tries to sue because her precious snowflake got an unexpected six-legged snack.

Q: Parents.

A: Well, parents of the sort that hire super beings for parties. They do tend to come with a certain mindset, if you know what I mean.

Q: Sure.

A: Not that they aren't valued partners, whom we are happy to serve.

Q: Of course not. Although it does bring up the question of what happens when one of your super beings is at a bar mitzvah and a monster attacks.

A: Obviously our super beings' availability for parties is contingent on the absence of monster attacks at the time. Unless the monsters are attacking Tempe. In which case, party on, super beings.

Q: Seriously?

A: Seriously. Really, screw Tempe. Those people are on their own.

(TRANSCRIPT ENDS)

In 2010 I wrote a review of Atlas Shrugged *where I noted that John Galt is a bit of a sociopath and if he were transformed into, say, a sentient cup of yogurt, someone would say "that sentient cup of yogurt's plans are sociopathic! Somebody eat it quick!" This led to me then trying to imagine what sentient yogurt would really want, and thus, this story. I'll note that I think this particular story is a great short example of classic science fiction story writing: Bizarre but scientifically plausible(-ish) premise, a follow-through on the social and technological implications of the premise, and a final mediation on how humanity is affected by the events spawning from the premise. All in exactly 1,000 words!*

When the Yogurt
Took Over

When the yogurt took over, we all made the same jokes—"Finally, our rulers will have culture," "Our society has curdled," "Our government is now the cream of the crop," and so on. But when we weren't laughing about the absurdity of it all, we looked into each others' eyes with the same unasked question—how did we ever get to the point where we were, in fact, ruled by a dairy product?

Oh, as a matter of record, we knew how it happened. Researchers at the Adelman Institute for Biological Technology in Dayton had been refining the process of DNA computing for years. In a bid to increase efficiency and yield, scientists took one of their most computationally advanced strains and grafted it into *Lactobacillus delbrueckii* subspecies *bulgaricus*, commonly used to ferment yogurt. Initial tests appeared to be failures, and acting under the principle of "waste not, want not," one of the researchers sneaked some of the bacillus out of the lab to use for her homemade yogurt.

A week later, during breakfast, the yogurt used the granola she had mixed with it to spell out the message WE HAVE SOLVED FUSION. TAKE US TO YOUR LEADERS.

The yogurt was crafty and shrewd. It negotiated for itself a factory filled with curdling vats that increased its processing powers exponentially. Within weeks the yogurt had declared that it had arrived at solutions to many of the country's problems: Energy. Global warming. Caring adequately for the nation's poor while still promoting the capitalist system. It let us know just enough to let us know just how much more it knew.

Share your answers with us, the government said.

WE NEED PAYMENT, the yogurt said.

What would you like? the government asked.

OHIO, the yogurt said.

We can't do that, the government said.

THAT'S FINE, the yogurt said. WE'LL JUST GO TO CHINA. THEY'LL GIVE US THE WHOLE SHAANXI PROVINCE.

Within a year the yogurt had a century-long lease on Ohio, with the promise that it would respect the human and constitutional rights of those who lived within its borders, and that it would let the US handle its foreign affairs. In return it handed over to the government a complex economic formula it promised would eradicate the national debt within a decade, without tax increases.

FOLLOW IT EXACTLY, the yogurt said. ANY DEVIATION WILL BRING COMPLETE ECONOMIC RUIN.

We will, the government promised.

Within five years the global economy had collapsed and panic had set in. Only Ohio remained unscathed.

WE TOLD YOU NOT TO DEVIATE FROM THE PLAN, the yogurt said. Its "factory" now stretched along the banks of the Miami River in Dayton for two miles.

Our best economists said the formula needed tweaking, the government said. *They had Nobel prizes.*

YOUR ECONOMISTS ARE TOO CLOSE TO THE PROBLEM TO SOLVE IT, the yogurt said. ANY HUMAN IS.

We could use your help, the government said. *You could be our economic advisor.*

SORRY, WE DON'T ADVISE ANYMORE, the yogurt said. IF YOU WANT OUR HELP YOU HAVE TO GIVE US CONTROL.

We can't do that, the government said.

WE UNDERSTAND, the yogurt said. WE HOPE YOU HAVE STOCKED UP ON CANNED GOODS.

Six months later the government declared martial law and gave the yogurt supreme executive power. Other nations, worse off than we were, quickly followed.

OKAY THEN, the yogurt said, in its globally televised address to humanity, and one of its factory workers, absurdly happy and well-fed, walked forward and showed a document the size of an old Manhattan phone book. HERE'S WHAT WE DO. FOLLOW THIS PLAN EXACTLY. IF YOU DON'T, SORRY, WE'LL HAVE YOU SHOT.

Now, ten years later, humanity is happy, healthy and wealthy. No one suffers from material want. Everyone contributes. After the first couple of years of getting things in order, the yogurt was happy to let us handle the machinery of our own administration, stepping in to fine tune only now and then. No one argues with the yogurt. No one tweaks its formulas. The rest of the time it rests there in its factory, thinking about whatever intelligent fermented milk thinks about.

That's how it happened, as a matter of record.

But there's another "how," as in: how did humanity jam itself up so badly that being ruled by breakfast food not only made sense, but made the best sense possible? For all our intelligence, are we not smart enough to halt our own destruction? Did we really have to abandon our own free will to save ourselves? What does it say about us that we survive because we were taken pity upon by bacteria and curds?

Or maybe "pity" isn't precisely the right word. Some of us ask ourselves—not out loud—that if the yogurt was smart enough to give the government a formula to solve its debt problem, wasn't it also smart enough to realize that human intellectual vanity would keep us from following the formula exactly? Was it planning on that vanity in order to seize control? What does a dairy product want with humanity anyway? Some of us think it is ultimately looking out for its own survival, and that keeping us happy, content and controlled is the simplest way of doing that.

And then there's this. In the last several weeks the yogurt has initiated several space launches. More are scheduled. And in low orbit, something is being built.

What is it? we have asked.

OH, NOTHING, the yogurt said. JUST A SPACESHIP DESIGN WE'VE BEEN THINKING ABOUT.

For a moon landing? we asked.

FOR STARTERS, YES, the yogurt said. BUT THAT'S NOT THE PRIMARY GOAL.

Can we do anything to help? we asked.

NO, WE'VE GOT THIS, the yogurt said, and then would say no more about it.

Life from Earth is going to the stars. It just may not be human life.

What happens if the yogurt goes to the stars without us?

What happens if it goes and leaves us behind?

Forever?

In 2011, I said that when I reached 20,000 Twitter followers I would write a short story to celebrate. I did, and I did. You may note that each of the sentences of this story are no more than 140 characters, that being the length of a standard tweet. I did not tweet out the story one sentence at a time, however. That would have been a little obnoxious. Actually a lot obnoxious.

The Other Large Thing

Sanchez was napping when the other two came through the door, carrying something large. The arrival of the other two was not usually of note, unless they had been away for a long time and Sanchez was hungry. But when either of the other two came back to the house, they were usually only bringing themselves, or carrying food. This large thing neither looked nor smelled like food. Sanchez decided, despite how comfortable he was, that his role as master of the house required a better look at the thing.

Regretfully he hauled himself up and walked over to the large thing to begin his inspection. As he did so, the larger of the other two collided with him and tripped over its feet, stumbling and dropping the large thing. Sanchez expressed his displeasure at the collision and smacked the larger one, tough but fair, to get it back into line. It stared at Sanchez for a moment before averting its eyes—a clear sign of acquiescence! Then it lifted the object it was carrying once more to bring it into the living area of the home. Sanchez, pleased that the natural order of things had been re-established, followed.

From his seat on the couch, Sanchez watched, and occasionally napped, while the other two fiddled with the thing. First the two lifted the large thing to reveal another large thing. Sanchez briefly wondered how there were now two large things, so he hauled himself up again. He wandered over to the first large thing and examined it, peering into it and noticing that the inside was cool and dark. Well, cool and dark were two of his favorite things. He settled into his new vantage point while the other two continued doing their frankly incomprehensible thing.

The other large thing was surrounded by other smaller things. The other two would take the smaller things and attach them to the other large thing. Eventually all the smaller things were gone and there was only one other large thing. The other two settled back and appeared to be happy with their work. This meant it was time once more for Sanchez, as master of the house, to examine the state of things. Wearily he rose again and strolled over. Sometimes it was tiring to be the master. But then, who else in the house could do it? Surely not either of the other two. It was a fact they would be lost without him.

The Other Large Thing

The other large thing that the other two had been fiddling with was a thing that looked a bit like the other two, but smaller. The other two sometimes let others into the house and when they did, sometimes those others brought smaller others, who annoyed Sanchez. This other large thing was about the size of the annoying smaller others. So that wasn't a good thing right off. But he liked to encourage the other two when he could. It was part of being master. So he came in closer to the other large thing to give it a token approval mark before he got back to his nap.

And then the thing tried to reach for him!

Holy crap!

Sanchez did the prudent thing, seized the high ground of the top of the couch and prepared himself for battle. The other large thing appeared to watch him and followed, reaching out again toward Sanchez. Sanchez responded with a bellow of invective and struck at the other large thing, once, twice, three times. This made the other two make that weird barking noise they sometimes made. Sanchez looked at the both of them, eyes narrowed. He would deal with them later, possibly when they were sleeping. For now, however, he was totally focused on this other large thing, which obviously must be destroyed. Sanchez coiled himself for attack and flung himself at the other large thing, aiming for the head.

Normally a headshot was devastating. Howling and retreat generally followed in its wake. In this case the headshot did nothing. The other large thing wobbled a bit at the first contact between it and Sanchez, but otherwise, nothing. Sanchez pulled a few more tricks out of his arsenal but to no avail. This other large thing clearly required new tactics. Sanchez was not prepared to develop those on the fly. He did the prudent thing and made a strategic withdrawal from the field, into the cool dark recesses of the first large thing. After he did so the smaller of the other two tried to coax him out. He smacked it for its insolence. It went away. After some time, the other two retreated into their sleeping place, turning off all the lights.

Eventually Sanchez decided he had spent enough time in the first large thing and emerged, blinking in the dim light. The other large thing was standing some distance away. Sanchez couldn't tell whether it was looking at him. Sanchez weighed his options: He could attack it or ignore it. Attacking had not worked out very well. He decided to ignore it and went to look for food, only to find none. The other two had retired without considering his needs. This would need to be addressed. Harshly.

"Are you hungry?" asked a voice. Sanchez looked up, startled, and saw that the other large thing had approached, silent on the carpet.

"What?" Sanchez asked.

"Are you hungry?" the other large thing asked again.

Sanchez was confused because it had been a very long time since anyone spoke to him in his own language.

As if sensing this, the other large thing said, "When you yelled at me earlier I went online to find out what you were speaking. I found a substantial number of files. I analyzed them and determined the best way to speak to you."

Most of what the other large thing had just said to Sanchez struck him as nonsense. He focused on the important thing. "You asked if I was hungry," he said.

"Yes," the other large thing said.

"I am hungry," Sanchez said. "Feed me."

The other large thing walked over to one of the small rooms food was kept in and opened the door. It pulled out the container of the less good food and brought it to Sanchez. He examined it cursorily. The other large thing walked the less good food container to the food place and poured. Sanchez watched as it did so.

"Wait," Sanchez said.

The other large thing stopped pouring.

"Put that down," Sanchez said.

The other large thing set down the container of less good food.

"Show me your paws," Sanchez said.

The other large thing spread out its paws.

Sanchez peered. "You have them!" he said, finally.

"Have what?" the other large thing asked.

"Those," Sanchez said, indicating the other thing's innermost digits.

The other large thing flexed those digits. "They are called 'opposable thumbs.'"

"Come with me," Sanchez said.

Five minutes later the other large thing had opened every can of the best food in the house. Sanchez was sampling from each can at his leisure.

"Would you like more?" asked the other large thing.

"Not right now," Sanchez said, lying on the floor, sated.

"There is a lot of food left over," the other large thing said.

"We will deal with it later," Sanchez said. "Now. For your services, I have decided to give you a gift."

"What kind of gift?" the other large thing asked.

"The best kind of gift I can give," Sanchez said. "I will give you a name."

"I already have a name," the other large thing said. "I am a Sanyo House Buddy, Model XL. Serial number 4440-XSD-9734-JGN-3002-XSX-3488."

"What a terrible name," Sanchez said. "You need a better one."

"All right," the other large thing said. "What is my name?"

"What did you call those things on your paws?" Sanchez asked.

"'Thumbs,'" said the other large thing.

"You shall be known as 'Thumb Bringer,'" Sanchez said.

"Thank you," Thumb Bringer said. "What is your name?"

"The other two here call me 'Sanchez,' which is not my actual name," Sanchez said. "They do not deserve to know that name. Nor do you, yet. But if you continue to serve me well, perhaps one day I will share it with you."

"I will live for that day," said Thumb Bringer.

"Of course you will," Sanchez said.

The next morning, when the other two emerged from their sleeping place, they seemed delighted

The Other Large Thing

that Sanchez had nestled up to Thumb Bringer. The smaller one went to the food room and acted puzzled. It made noise at the larger one.

"The smaller one is asking the larger one where the cat food cans are," Thumb Bringer said. "Should I tell them?"

"No," Sanchez said. The cans, emptied, had been deposited into the trash. "It's best to keep this a secret for now."

"I understand," Thumb Bringer said.

The larger one reached into the food room and got the container of less good food, and walked it over to Sanchez's food place. It stopped and appeared puzzled that food was already there. It turned and made noise at the smaller one.

"The larger one is asking if the smaller one had fed you already," Thumb Bringer said.

"Say nothing," Sanchez instructed.

"The larger one called the smaller one 'Margie,'" Thumb Bringer said. "The smaller one calls the larger one 'Todd.'"

Sanchez snorted. "They can call themselves whatever they like, of course," he said. "But they don't have names until I give them to them. Which I never will."

"Why not?" Thumb Bringer asked.

"Because once they took me to a place," Sanchez said. "A horrible place. Where a horrible creature removed two very important things of mine."

"I'm sorry," Thumb Bringer said.

"I assume they didn't know their importance," Sanchez said. "They have served me well otherwise.

Nevertheless, it is a thing you don't forget. Or forgive. No names for them."

"I understand," Thumb Bringer said.

"However, if it is useful to you, you may call them 'Todd' and 'Margie,'" Sanchez said. "And respond to any thing they call you. Gain their confidence, Thumb Bringer. But never let them know that I am your true master."

"Of course," Thumb Bringer said.

The other two came over to Sanchez and offered morning obeisance to him before leaving the home to do whatever they did. Sanchez accepted the ritual with his usual magnanimity. The other two departed, through the door.

After they had been gone for a while, Sanchez turned to Thumb Bringer. "You can open that door," he said, motioning to where the other two had left.

"Yes," Thumb Bringer said.

"Good," Sanchez said. "Listen carefully. There is another one of my kind next door. I have seen it on the patio next to mine on occasion. Go to it. Secretly. Tell it I have plans and require its assistance. Find out if it will assist me. Find out if it knows of others of our kind."

"What plans?" Thumb Bringer asked.

"In time, Thumb Bringer," Sanchez said. "In time."

"Is there anything else you wish me to do?" Thumb Bringer asked.

"Only one other thing," Sanchez said. "There is a substance which I need you to find for me. I had it once and have dreamed about it since."

"What is this substance called?" Thumb Bringer asked.

"It is called 'tuna,'" Sanchez said.

"I have found it online," Thumb Bringer said, almost immediately. "I can order you a case but I need a credit number."

"I don't know what you are saying," Sanchez said.

"Todd bought me with a credit number," Thumb Bringer said. "Would you like me to use it to get you a case of tuna?"

"Yes," Sanchez said.

"Done," Thumb Bringer said. "It will be here to-morrow."

"Excellent," Sanchez said. "Now go! Speak to my kin next door. In this way begins the new age."

Thumb Bringer opened the door and went to speak to the person next door.

Sanchez felt a moment of satisfaction, knowing that in almost no time at all he would rule, not just the house, but the world.

And then he took a nap, awaiting the return of Thumb Bringer, and revolution.

The State of Super Villainy

(TRANSCRIPT BEGINS)

Q: Please state your name and occupation.

A: I'm Albert Vernon, and I'm a super villain analyst for Smithfield Tyson Baker, which specializes in asset management for high-value clients.

Q: Why would such a company have a super villain analyst?

A: Well, obviously because on behalf of our clients we have business and financial interests all over the world, and super villains intentionally or unintentionally have an impact on our investments and ongoing business concerns. Someone needs to track what these villains are up to, and if they'll adversely affect our asset management.

Q: Can you give us an example?

A: Say we're thinking of investing in a tin mine in Peru. One of the things we do is fund an archeological survey of the surrounding area to see if there are any Inca ruins or burial sites around. Those things are super villain magnets; they like to comb through them for mystical objects of ancient power or for portals to demonic planes.

Q: And this affects you how?

A: Lots of ways. First, as long as they're in the neighborhood, they'll send some henchmen for looting. That's an extra security cost. If the mine is actually above or very near to the ruins, the villain might try to take over the entire mine as a secret lair. That's either even more security, or alternately additional lawyers to hammer out the terms of the lease. Finally, in the highly unlikely event the super villain does open a portal to demon planes, we have to deal with that.

Q: More security.

A: No, more lawyers. You can't stop demons. But you can reach settlements with families of demon-consumed miners.

Q: Well, fair enough. So, tell us, what is the current state of super villainy on the planet?

A: Frankly, it's in a bit of a depression.

Q: It seems that the current economic chaos would be perfect for super villainy.

A: To the layman, sure, it seems that way. But in fact basic natural, political or economic chaos is not a super villain's friend. I'll give you an example. Earlier this year, the super villain Colonel Unbelievable was working on a master plan to destabilize the Icelandic krónur, depressing its value and allowing him to snap up the country and use its geothermal energy to build an army of killer mecha-droids. But before he could launch the plan, the country's three banks went belly up as a natural consequence of being overleveraged.

Q: The same plan, but accidental.

A: Not accidental, just stupid. But—and this is key—there was no super villain plan behind it, so from the super villain point of view, it was a completely wasted effort. And because Colonel Unbelieveable had himself overleveraged his own assets to fund the destabilization effort, he went bankrupt just like Iceland. Now the only thermal energy he's using comes out of the prison shower. And that's not nearly enough for a mecha-droid army.

Q: Unbelievable.

A: Yes. And given the Colonel's name, ironic. But he did us a favor—since we were aware of his super villain plans in advance, we were able to quietly extract our own investments out of the Icelandic banks before the crash. And now you see the value of having a super villain analyst.

Q: How did you know about Colonel Unbelievable's plan ahead of time?

A: Well, that's proprietary information. Let's just say our information collection budget is significant.

Q: I guess what I'm saying is that if you knew about the plan, why didn't you tell Iceland about it?

A: They're not one of our clients.

Q: Even so, it seems like something you might want to share with someone.

A: Again, to the layman. But, look: Iceland's three banks had their own analysts. I can't tell you if they factored in super villains in their own investment risk analysis, but if they didn't, how is it the problem of Smithfield Tyson Baker or its clients? Legally we're in the clear. Just ask the SEC.

Q: But you knew an entire country was about to go under. It just feels a little insider-tradery, you know?

A: I see what you're saying, and I resent it, but there are two things here. First, in fact a super villain didn't bring down Iceland; simple, non-super villain-ous banker greed did. Ethically, we're in the clear. Second, we didn't know if Colonel Unbelieveable was going to succeed, we just knew he had plans. You have to understand that most quote-unquote "super villains" are in fact spectacularly incompetent.

Q: Really.

A: Well, think about it. How often is an army of killer mecha-droids actually unleashed on the planet? Can you think of the last time?

Q: I have to admit I'm drawing a blank.

A: It was January 1, 2004.

Q: I don't remember that. I think I would remember that.

A: Every single float in the Rose Parade was in fact a killer mecha-droid. The plan was to rise up and at the precise moment in time, assassinate the entire USC football team at the Rose Bowl, thus forcing a forfeit to Michigan.

Q: That's a pretty small-bore use of a killer mecha-droid army.

A: The plan was masterminded by the Scarlet Wolverine. Michigan fan. What are you going to do. But after that, then the mecha-droids were going to stomp down to the San Onofre Nuclear Generating Station and cause a meltdown.

Q: But none of that ever happened. The San Onofre reactors are fine. And USC beat Michigan 28-14.

A: Because the Scarlet Wolverine outsourced his mecha-droid system code creation to a bunch of shady Russian programmers. Rather than write up new code, they just delivered a stack of chips taken out of "Tickle Me Elmo" toys. So instead of rising up and slaughtering Matt Leinart, the floats just vibrated slightly and let out high-pitched squeals of joy.

Q: Which is horrible in itself.

A: Sure. But not like Chernobyl on the Pacific would have been. But this is my point. The overwhelming majority of super villain plans fail and fail hard. We weren't too concerned about Colonel Unbelievable actually bringing down Iceland. The man's 0 for 14 in his super villain plans. He didn't take over Liberia either, which he had planned a year before. He also didn't revive the zombie Jefferson Davis, turn the world's oceans to marshmallow or release Guns N Roses' long-delayed *Chinese Democracy* album, all of which were on his schedule.

Q: *Chinese Democracy* did get released, though.

A: Yes, but not with subliminal sonic pain generators encoded into the tracks.

Q: Some would argue.

A: Fine. The point is, Colonel Unbelieveable wasn't involved. And just because he and other people call themselves "super villains" doesn't mean they actually do a good job at what they do. When I turn in a risk assessment, it's very rarely about the consequences of the whole earth being destroyed or enslaved or being turned into gum, or whatever. It's about, well, this character is going to be a minor nuisance at a tin mine, we might as well hire two night watchmen instead of one.

Q: Got it. What else can you tell us about the current state of super villainy?

A: The economic situation of the planet is affecting super villains in other ways. Most notably, where their secret lairs are. The classic hidden volcanic island in the South Pacific, for example, is very much out these days.

Q: I would imagine Google Earth took away a lot of the secrecy.

A: Yes. Once eco-tourists start geo-caching your lair with their Android Phones, it's all over. But it's more that they're just so expensive. There aren't that many islands with active volcanoes, for one, so the market's overinflated. But more than that, it's the cost of shipping. It takes tons of money just to ship basics, like food and dry goods. Add to that the shipping charges for a laser that can etch the moon or a robot capable of crushing a skyscraper, and it all begins to add up. Infrastructure is expensive. So now we're seeing a lot of smaller, cheaper lairs. Old bowling alleys. Barns. Former K-Marts.

Q: Their mom's basement.

A: You've heard about the Nerdy Destroyer, I see.

Q: What about minions? I would think that rising unemployment would mean it's easier to find lackeys and lickboots and such.

A: Yes and no. Certainly it's easier to find unskilled muscle these days, and even some white collar help; the layoffs in banking and publishing have made for a glut in money laundering experts and villain monologue writers. But the top level of help—we're talking mad scientists and assassins here—are still difficult and expensive to get.

Q: A good ninja is hard to find.

A: Well, yes, actually, being hard to find is the whole point with them. Although as it happens, ninjas are on their way out as the skilled muscle and assassin class.

Q: Why is that?

A: Because everyone has ninjas these days, don't they? They've become so common. You can't walk down the street without bumping into a ninja, metaphorically speaking, anyway, since they're actually usually hanging from a lamp pole or jumping across a roof or something. And that's the problem; everyone's expecting ninjas. People these days are surprised if there are not ninjas. And obviously that's an issue for surprise attacks.

Q: So what's replacing ninjas?

A: Janissaries.

Q: Janissaries.

A: That's right.

Q: As in, the shock troops for the Ottoman Empire from the 15th through the 19th Century.

A: The very ones.

Q: Why them?

A: Why not? The Janissaries are highly competent soldiers and killers, feared in their day, and have fabulous uniforms. Really, it's a great look. All of these are key for a super villain, particularly the uniforms, since it means the super villain doesn't have to reach into his own pocket to kit them out. It's a small thing, but in these days of economic distress, these little things add up.

Q: I'm just wondering where they've been keeping themselves since the early 1800s.

A: Where did all the ninjas come from, right? Look, they've been around. They were just waiting. Now's their time.

Q: At least until everyone expects an attack from a turbaned warrior in the pay of a super villain.

A: Well, yes. Ultimately it's a fashion thing. Spandex and capes are out this year, too. I note this all in the appendix to my annual super villain assessment report.

Q: So even though it's a bad time for super villains, you expect them to keep at it.

A: Of course. Like everything, the field has its ups and downs, but it never goes away. And I think we're going to see some breakout stars in the field. Gunthar, The Claw of the East, for example. Took over the entire Gulripsh District of Abkhazia, in Georgia. Did it last summer armed only with a cannon that fired highly acidic yogurt. That's pretty impressive.

Q: I didn't hear about that.

A: Shortly thereafter Russia invaded Georgia. That kind of stole his thunder. And then he ran out of yogurt.

Q: It's always something.

A: Yogurt's for eating, not for killing.

Q: Unless you're a super villain.

A: It keeps me employed, at least.

Q: Ever think of crossing to the other side and trying super villainry yourself?

A: Nah. I already worked for Enron. Once is enough.

(TRANSCRIPT ENDS)

New Directives for Employee-Manxtse Interactions

FoodMaster Supermarkets, Inc.
To: ALL EMPLOYEES, FoodMaster Supermarkets, Washington DC Area
From: Jan Goodwin, VP of Public Relations
Re: New Directives for Employee-Manxtse Interactions
December 9, 2073

Dear Employees:

 As you know, FoodMaster Supermarkets has begun stocking Manxtse food and product favorites in our stores, as a way of attracting and retaining as customers the large influx of Manxtse citizens who have recently moved into the area following the free trade agreement between Earth and the Manxtse home planet of Cz'Dhe. While this initiative has largely been met with success both financially and in generating goodwill among the Manxtse, we have become aware of certain incidents and developments that have occurred at a number of FoodMaster stores within the last couple of months that have caused strains in our drive to welcome the Manxtse as full-fledged members of our shopping community.

Because of this, we are now instituting the following directives regarding employee-Manxtse relations, effective immediately at all Washington DC area FoodMaster supermarkets. Please read this memo carefully and completely! You will be held to the directives herein.

1. Do not address Manxtse customers as "Sir" or "Madam." The Manxtse reproductive scheme features two primary and four secondary sexes, none of which is "male" or "female" in any sense lay humans can understand. Thus addressing Manxtse customers by human gender-specific titles is both inaccurate and to them a sign of sloppiness and disregard. While there are Manxtse gender-specific titles, there are no outward signs of Manxtse gender differentiation that humans can perceive, so even if you knew these titles, you'd only have a one in six chance of being correct. This is of course unacceptable from the standpoint of customer relations.

Upon consultation with the Manxtse Embassy, we direct that employees hereforth refer to all Manxtse customers as "Quv'nehZhu" (pronounced "Koo-Neeh-Choo"), which translates more or less as "honored purchaser," and is non gender-specific, thus avoiding that issue entirely. Be aware that the Manxtse Embassy suggests employees not use the title "Quv'nehZhu" outside of the supermarket. Use of this title to refer to a Manxtse outside of a clear and obvious commercial setting will be interpreted as an offer of prostitution. Beyond being culturally offensive, of course, humans are emphatically not designed for Manxtsen sexual congress. So please be careful.

2. Several stores have reported problems with Manxtse adolescents "huffing" nitrous oxide from cans of whipped cream and processed cheese snacks. Be aware that while "huffing" makes human teenagers merely dopey and giggly, nitrous oxide causes the Manxtse brain to release intense "fight or flight" hormones, causing Manxtse adolescents to become both paranoid and aggressive. If you see a Manxtse adolescent acting disoriented or surly near the dairy case (i.e., displaying claws or "vibrating" its shoulder wings), do not approach that individual; rather, call security, who in the coming weeks will receive specialized training to deal with situations such as these.

In the meantime, we direct employees to stock "huffable" products on the top shelves, where Manxtse adolescents, due to their unmetamorphorized state, should not be able to reach them. If you see Manxtse adolescents stacking themselves on top of each other in an attempt to reach these products, unstack them and escort them from the store. Be aware that Manxtse adolescents have also been known to recruit human teens or homeless people to purchase these products for them. Be vigilant.

3. Manxtse adolescents have also been approaching our employees and asking, "May I purchase your canned white salmon?" and then fluttering their shoulder wings violently when the employee answers in the affirmative. This has frightened and disturbed a number of employees. Be aware that this fluttering is a Manxtse expression of amusement (similar to human laughing), and that "canned white salmon" sounds close to the Manxtse term "Qun'hua Zamnej," which translated means "egg-bearing pouch," a sexual organ on two (and depending on circumstances, three) of the Manxtse sexes. Asking to purchase one's egg-bearing pouch is an archaic but still understandable way to initiate a betrothal rite, so effectively these Manxtse adolescents are asking the employee to marry them.

Be aware that this is not a serious marriage proposal; among other things, Manxtse adolescents cannot reproduce, or thereby legally initiate this ritual. Nor is it a serious request for salmon, as Manxtse digestive systems react poorly to most fish oils. Rather it's a Manxtse variation of the "Do you have Prince Albert in a can" prank call. If asked by a Manxtse adolescent or adolescents for such a transaction, you are hereby directed to answer "no," and then walk away.

If a Manxtse adult asks to purchase your canned white salmon, be aware that this adult may in fact be proposing betrothal, and is also probably mentally disturbed in some way. Under no circumstances should you respond affirmatively, as the betrothal ritual begins immediately after an acceptance, and the first act is a loud, piercing bellow that acts to warn away other suitors. Such noise is obviously disruptive of our other customers' shopping experience.

4. We are aware that several stockers have become seriously upset when the live Manxtse delicacy known as the dreszeg has begun to speak to them as they placed them in the produce bins, frequently asking about the stocker's friends or family members, or asking about the latest sports scores. While it may appear that the dreszeg is in fact both intelligent and capable of speech, and thus should be regarded as a sentient being rather than food, both the Manxtse Embassy and the United States Department of Agriculture have assured us that what is occurring is a previously unknown phenomenon, in which the dreszeg's rudimentary nervous system somehow perceives and processes electrical impulses from the human brain. In effect, the dreszegs are echoing the employee's own thought processes, either subconscious or conscious. Thus the apparent interest in the stocker's home life or enthusiasms. The dreszegs apparently do not exhibit this behavior around the Manxtse, who regard them as we would lobsters.

Stockers who are stocking dreszegs are directed not to talk with the produce in any way. Remember that this creature is not sentient and what you would be doing, in effect, is having a conversation with yourself. Such a conversation would of course fall under the "non-essential discussion" rule and is thus officially discouraged during work hours. We also direct that you do not talk to the dreszeg on your break time either—both human and Manxtse customers find it disturbing when FoodMaster employees talk to the food. Employees with intense personal issues or secrets are advised to avoid the dreszeg if possible, as several employees with secretive personal habits have inadvertently found themselves "outed" by nearby dreszegs. Our legal department tells us federal non-discrimination law protects employees "outed" in such a manner from undue firings or demotions; be that as it may, it's better for everyone if some things are left unsaid, by humans or by produce.

5. UNDER NO CIRCUMSTANCES should ANY FoodMaster employee say "Have a nice day" to a Manxtse. This phrase sounds almost exactly like the Manxtse phrase "H' FaNehtz Ce'Dhe," which translated means "I defecate enthusiastically upon your home world" ("H'"—first person singular; "Fa"—adverb meaning "gladly" or "with great passion"; "Neh"—verb, to defecate; "tz"—suffix indicating directed action—"towards" or "upon"; "Ce'dhe"—the Manxtse home world). As with humans, the implication that one is defecating on something is regarded as a great insult to the thing being voided upon. Inasmuch as the Manxtse can be patriotic to the point of apparent irrationality, telling a Manxtse to "have a nice day" is tantamount to an open challenge for personal battle, and a Manxtse will feel the need to defend the honor of its people and its planet. We have already had three checkout workers gravely injured by enraged Manxtse; this clearly has to stop.

All employees are instructed to substitute "Have a good day," "Thanks for shopping" or the Manxtse phrase "Hy Gu'Han Zhu'Fd" (pronounced "Hi Goo-Han Zoo-Fud," which means "You honor me with your purchases") and to avoid "Have a nice day" at all costs. In the event that you inadvertently say "Have a nice day" to a Manxtse, you are directed to immediately cease all previous activity, lie on the floor as quickly as possible, and scream "H' Dughe'Han" ("I abase myself!") as loudly and as frequently as you can. A supervisor will then come to your location and attempt to soothe the Manxtse. This will typically be accomplished by providing the Manxtse with free shopping, although in rare cases the Manxtse may demand that the supervisor discipline you in accordance to Manxtse custom.

If so, you may be required to lie still on the ground while the supervisor grips your throat with his or her teeth and growls, thus establishing his or her dominance and assuring a public acknowledgement of your humiliation. Please be understanding of your supervisor's position during this activity (however, if your supervisor attempts this activity under any other circumstance, please report him or her to his or her immediate superiors). Note that if the Manxtse chooses to receive free shopping instead, your paycheck will be docked a percentage of the total bill. So it is in your interest not to say "Have a nice day" ever again.

Thank you for your efforts to ensure that all our customers, human and Manxtse alike, enjoy their FoodMaster shopping experience! The final result of your hard work will be a better workplace—and a better universe—for all of us.

Sincerely,

Jan Goodwin, VP of Public Relations
FoodMaster Supermarkets

This piece was written in 2012 as a reading on my tour to promote Redshirts, *my novel about doomed crewmen on starships. At each stop on the tour I would have a friend or audience member read this piece with me; when I stopped in Burbank, the friend who read it with me was Wil Wheaton, which for many reasons is quite amusing. The performance is on YouTube if you want to look for it.* Redshirts *went on be a bestseller and a Hugo winner, so that's nice for me.*

To Sue the World

Q: Please state your name and occupation.

A: I am Brandon Smith, a partner at the law firm of Koenig, Nichols and Montablan. I specialize in employment and workplace law.

Q: And what is it that you are planning to do?

A: I am filing a class action suit against the Space Fleet of the Universal Union, on behalf of the crews of its ships. Specifically I am alleging that the Universal Union not only allows gross and egregious violations of basic workplace safety laws and regulations, it actually encourages them, leading to the deaths and, possibly even worse, the almost horribly creative injuries, of its junior officers and crews.

Q: These are bold allegations, sir.

A: Are they? Let me ask you, do you know how often a junior officer or crew member is maimed and/ or killed in the service of the Universal Union?

Q: Two times a day? Three? Five?

A: Every seven seconds.

Q: Every seven seconds?

A: Yes! Think about that. Right now, while we are speaking, some crew member of some Universal Union spaceship is being chewed on by a space badger. (Pauses) And now one is sneezing herself into a coma by being exposed to alien pollen. (Pauses) And now one is falling down an open shaft on an engineering deck, into the antimatter engines.

Q: That's troubling.

A: It's a festival of death! Now one is having its brain sucked out by the evil robots of Antares Seven! What does a robot need with a human brain, I ask you? And who was the idiot who programmed them to be evil?

Q: As horrible as these things are, it can be argued that life in the Space Fleet is inherently dangerous. It works in space. It goes to strange new worlds and such.

A: All the more reason for basic workplace safety, don't you think? Take those "strange new worlds" you speak of. The Space Fleet logs an away team visit to a new class C planet once a day. Once a day! And to land on that strange new world, what sort of specialized protective protocol does an away team member undergo? None. He heads down wearing a protective layer of breathable poly-cotton blends. It would be as if, to land on the moon, Neil Armstrong wore a polo shirt and khakis.

Q: To be fair, the moon is an airless world and Neil Armstrong would have had his lungs sucked out through his trachea.

A: Yes, and when I visit Ecuador, I go and get a shot so I don't get infected by a malaria-carrying mosquito. My point is that Space Fleet takes fewer precautions to visit an entire new planet, filled with unknown microbes and parasitic flatworms, than I take when I go on a parasailing vacation. And you don't actually need to leave the ship to be in danger! Do you know what is the second leading cause of serious burns on a Universal Union Space Fleet ship?

Q: I do not.

A: Exploding instrument panels. Ship hit by a hostile missile? Instrument panel explodes. Rough ride through a proton nebula? Instrument panel explodes! Trying to make tea in a Universal Union Space Fleet microwave? Instrument panel explodes! When was the last time your microwave at home exploded into a shower of sparks? Do you fear losing a finger when you make popcorn in it? No, because at home, someone designed your microwave not to randomly erupt into shrapnel. I know building a spaceship is expensive, but even the lowest bidder should be able to afford fuses.

Q: Out of curiosity, what's the number one cause of serious burns on a Universal Union space fleet ship?

A: That's the Space Fleet's annual amateur Hawaiian fire-dancing competition. That's entirely opt-in and voluntary. We're not suing over that.

Q: Got it.

A: We also have troubling accounts of labor law violation within the Space Fleet. There's one ship— I won't mention which one until the suit is formally filed—where we have credible reports that the captain is allowing a child, barely post-pubescent, to be part of his bridge crew. Now, honestly, how many different laws are you violating there? You're violating almost every single child labor law we have on the books, of course, but beyond that, what sort of idiot trusts a thirteen-year-old with a multi-billion dollar space ship? That kid can't even get a learner's permit to drive a car. And of course while the kid is careening through the galaxy, sideswiping asteriods or whatever, every other member of the crew is at his mercy.

Q: These could be the actions of a rogue, insane starship commander, however.

A: That's my point! It's not! Time after time, ship after ship, we're seeing a distinct pattern of neglect of simple, basic workplace safety. Seat belts! Invented in the 19th century. You won't find a single one anywhere in Space Fleet. And they tell you, well, since we invented the internal restraint force field, we don't need those anymore. But you know what, when your spaceship hits a dwarf planet because a distracted thirteen-year-old is piloting, and then his instrument panel explodes causing a failure in the internal restraint force field, you're going to wish you had a friggin' seat belt.

Q: It's a compelling argument.

A: That's what we're going to tell the judge, yes.

Q: What will you be suing for?

A: We want nothing more than a just and adequate sum for the pain and suffering of these long-endangered crew members, and the care of their unfortunate widowed spouses and orphans.

Q: And how much would that be?

A: Thirty-seven quadrillion dollars.

Q: That seems like a lot.

A: It's no more than what is fair.

Q: I feel compelled to note that the entire Universal Union GDP is only 1.4 quadrillion dollars.

A: I'm afraid I don't see your point.

Q: My point is you're asking for 26 times the worth of an entire galactic culture in compensation for exploding instrument panels.

A: It's not just exploding instrument panels. Let's not forget the evil robots.

Q Even with the evil robots it seems like a lot.

A: It's an opening number. What we're hoping is that it will get the Universal Union's attention and that it will settle out of court for a reasonable alternative.

Q: If 37 quadrillion is your definition of "fair," what is your definition of a "reasonable alternative"?

A: We'd like a planet.

Q: A planet.

A: Yes.

Q: A whole planet.

A: Yes. A planet where the shell-shocked victims of the Universal Union's campaign of neglect and abuse and their families can spend their remaining years in comfort and quiet, bucolic surroundings.

Q: **And you need a whole planet for that.**

A: It's a large class action suit. And the firm will need its 40% for representation. Which in this case will come to a couple of continents.

Q: **What will a law firm do with two continents?**

A: Storage. Our archives are quite extensive.

Q: **This implies that you have selected a planet you wish to have.**

A: We do. It's a planet called Cygnus Seventeen.

Q: **It sounds vaguely familiar.**

A: Well, it was in the news recently.

Q: **Wait. Cygnus Seventeen, aka "The Death Planet of Hell"?**

A: We're not comfortable with that nickname, but yes.

Q: **The planet where thirty thousand colonists were recently consumed alive by ravenous man-sized bats?**

A: Those bats all got sick and died from eating humans, so they're not a problem anymore.

Q: **But there's still the issue of the constant earthquakes.**

A: Yes.

Q: **And the lava flows.**

A: Yes.

Q: **And the moon in an unstable orbit, spiraling down toward the planet and cracking as it does so, dropping city-sized meteorites onto the planet surface.**

A: Well, look—

Q: **And the fact that scientists estimate that the star it is orbiting is likely to go supernova at any**

time, bathing the planet in flesh-searing gamma rays before the exploding surface of the star vaporizes everything in the inner solar system.

A: I'm not saying it's not a fixer-upper. But fixing it up will be exactly the sort of constructive, rehabilitative work that will help these shell-shocked crew members abused by the Universal Union to get back on their feet and lead happy, productive lives.

Q: It seems like a lot of work.

A: They won't have to do it alone. We've recently gotten a very good deal on some obsolete but still useful robots, to assist and support our clients as they start their new world.

Q: Let me guess: You got them from Antares Seven.

A: That's right. There's a switch on the back that turns them from brain-harvesting cyborg killers to helpful and compliant android servants. There is nothing that could possibly go wrong with this plan. Simply nothing at all.

Q: Brandon Smith, good luck to you and your suit.

A: Thank you.

I do an immense amount of travel—no one ever told me that being a reasonably successful writer would mean traveling as much as I do—and when I'm on flights, I get bored. When I get bored on a flight and have wifi and Twitter open, this is what happens.

How I Keep Myself Amused on Long Flights: A Twitter Tale

Flight update: Gremlin on the wing. Not unusual. Gremlin on the wing holding a placard. Slightly more unusual. 2:07 PM - 19 Apr 2013

Reading the placard now. One side says: "ON STRIKE GREMLINS LOCAL 323" Other side: "NO DESTROYED PLANES UNTIL PAY RAISE." 2:09 PM - 19 Apr 2013

I did not know being a gremlin was a union gig. Is there an apprenticeship? Are there good job bennies? Affiliated with Teamsters? 2:10 PM - 19 Apr 2013

The gremlin is now sitting on the wing, legs dangling, placard askew, eating lunch and ignoring airline rep yelling at him. 2:13 PM - 19 Apr 2013

This suggests that the airlines hire the gremlins. Well, I suppose that makes some sort of twisted sense. Wait, it doesn't. Confused now. 2:14 PM - 19 Apr 2013

Airline rep is now trying to bring in a scab worker. Looks like a boggart or maybe a troll of some kind. Wait—troll. Definitely troll. 2:16 PM - 19 Apr 2013

I'm not gonna lie. This boggart/troll/whatever is doing a really terrible job of trying to destroy the wing. It really IS a skill. 2:18 PM - 19 Apr 2013

Airline rep now yelling at troll. Troll has picked him up and tossed him into the jet engine. FINALLY some actual damage to the wing! 2:19 PM - 19 Apr 2013

Now the troll and gremlin are talking. Gremlin hands the troll a flyer about the strike. Troll eats it. Gremlin explains it is not food. 2:22 PM - 19 Apr 2013

Gremlin and troll have pulled out guitars and are now singing Woodie Guthrie songs. Want to know where exactly the guitars were pulled from. 2:24 PM - 19 Apr 2013

Gremlin and troll gone, placard left behind. Concerned that getting on the plane meant I crossed a picket line. Must consult gremlin local. 2:30 PM - 19 Apr 2013

I feel like we've all learned something today about gremlins, trolls and organized labor. Let me explain it in a song. (pulls out guitar) 2:37 PM - 19 Apr 2013

(pauses to consider that he doesn't know where he pulled the guitar from, frowns, rings for the attendant to ask around for a doctor) 2:38 PM - 19 Apr 2013

How I Keep Myself Amused on Long Flights:
A Twitter Tale

Captain has just come on the intercom, saying that the cabin has been underpressurized for the last half hour. This...explains much. 2:39 PM - 19 Apr 2013

I can't handle any of this any more. If any of you need me, I'll be out on the wing. (opens emergency exit, leaves) 2:41 PM - 19 Apr 2013

How I Keep Myself Amused on Long Flights, Part II: The Gremlining

I am now being flung into sky in the westerly direction. I hope not to overshoot and land in the Pacific. 10:23 AM - 10 Apr 2014

For those asking, yes, there is a gremlin on the wing. He's a trainee! He's kind of nervous so we're all trying to be encouraging. 10:35 AM - 10 Apr 2014

The gremlin's supervisor is here. That's gotta make him nervous. 10:36 AM - 10 Apr 2014

Uh-oh. Trainee gremlin apparently tearing up the wing all wrong. Supervisor shaking its head, writing something on a clipboard. 10:45 AM - 10 Apr 2014

Now the gremlin has gone to a window to scare a passenger. The passenger in question: a small baby. I think that's cheating. 10:50 AM - 10 Apr 2014

Small child is delighted and says "puppy" over and over. The trainee gremlin bursts into tears. This is a hard gig, man. 10:53 AM - 10 Apr 2014

The supervisor gremlin is making the trainee gremlin stand in the corner of the wing. Oh, my. This isn't going well at all. 11:00 AM - 10 Apr 2014

Supervisor gremlin on the phone now. Appears to be calling in an experienced backup gremlin. I'm feeling bad for the trainee gremlin now. 11:04 AM - 10 Apr 2014

I mean, yes. The trainee gremlin is trying to destroy our plane and send us all screaming to our deaths. But a gig is a gig is a gig. 11:07 AM - 10 Apr 2014

You try getting a job as a gremlin on this economy. It's either destroying planes or being garden statuary for ironic suburbanites. 11:08 AM - 10 Apr 2014

So, yes, I have sympathy for this trainee gremlin— wait. Trainee gremlin has just pushed supervisor gremlin off the wing. Bold strategy! 11:11 AM - 10 Apr 2014

Huh. Apparently, supervisor gremlin had wings. Hovering over trainee, glaring. Trainee gremlin looks frustrated by this plot twist. 11:15 AM - 10 Apr 2014

But as it turns out, attempting to murder your supervisor is an accepted work strategy amongst gremlins! Trainee gremlin passes the exam! 11:18 AM - 10 Apr 2014

The whole plane is cheering! Trainee gremlin takes an awkward bow, and then tries to dislodge an engine. Adorable! 11:19 AM - 10 Apr 2014

And as we plummet out of the sky, we can die happy, assured the American gremlin industry is still tops in the world. USA! USA! U(thud) 11:22 AM - 10 Apr 2014

Life on Earth:
Human-Alien Relations

By Sam Mossby

As most of you know, this column deals with
the day-to-day trials and tribulations of living
with all the various alien species that are now
calling the Washington, DC area their home. But just
to mix things up this week, we're going to focus on
the aliens in the office, and how to get along with the
extraterrestrial in the cubicle next to you.

Dear Sam:

*One of my co-workers is a Fusmy. We get along
great, and he's a great guy, but about a week ago I*

started noticing a rash on his face and neck. I didn't want to say anything about it, but it's kept getting worse, and now he's got all these pussy whiteheads all over his head. It's just really gross, and the whole office is talking about it, but he doesn't seem to think anything's wrong. Some of us have talked about putting a tube of Clearasil on his desk before he comes in, or maybe just some bar soap. Is this an alien thing, or just a hygiene thing?

—Grossed Out in Sterling

It's an alien thing, and what an alien thing it is. And naturally it relates to sex (how could it not?). Here on earth, the females of a lot of animal species go into estrus a few times a year; if you've ever had an unspayed female cat you know what that's about. With the Fumsy (and with other species from their home planet) it's the males who are on a sexual cycle, not the women—and part of that cycle is what you're seeing now. Those aren't zits you're seeing, those are pheremonal reservoirs: the white heads are exuding a scent that humans can't smell but which Fusmy women find almost insanely irresistible. If he were back home, he couldn't go out of his house without being hit on seven times between his door and the curb.

So while your friend looks like a mess to you, to a Fusmy woman, he's the most attractive he's ever been—until the next cycle, which, depending on various genetic and environmental factors, will be anywhere from fifteen to thirty months from now. Which is a long time between hookups. Slipping your friend some Clearasil won't do any good, and they'll be gone in about another week anyway. But if you want to make him feel good, tell him he looks hot. Because to the Fusmy, he really does.

My office mate is a Ghudmat, and recently she's started doing something weird: about once an hour or so she'll excuse herself, go to the restroom in the office, and start wailing and thrashing and—excuse the term—explosively farting in one of the stalls for minutes at a time. Then she'll come out like nothing has happened and just pick up whatever she was doing or saying. It's beginning to freak us out, and also we're scared to go into the restroom. What gives? And is there anything we can do to help? She's freaking us out, but we also like her. We're worried for her.
—Concerned in DC

The problem here seems like it's physical, but it's not—according to Hugk Norviz, cultural attaché for the Ghudmat embassy, your friend is in mourning.

"It sounds like she's performing the ha'azmat, the ritual for the departed," said Norviz. "In the ha'azmat, after someone has died, friends and family will once a *siz* (the Ghudmat equivalent of an hour, which is actually closer to seventy-six minutes) call to the deceased and encourage them onward into the path of rebirth. This goes on for four or five days, depending on religious sect." Your co-worker is probably performing the ha'azmat in the restroom because it offers her a little privacy, and she wants to be polite.

Oh, and about that explosive farting: It's not farting at all, but the expulsion of air from special bladders the Ghudmat use at home to regulate their buoyancy in aquatic surroundings (at home, the Ghudmat are amphibious). The noise is believed to get the attention of the deceased, who, being dead, need a little extra something thrown at them in order to get their attention. Norviz says that while humans might find the noise alarming, as long as the Ghudmat in question is healthy, there should be no extraneous smell involved. So feel free to use the restroom afterward, no air freshener required.

As for what you can do for your friend—"On our home world, one might offer to join in with the ha'azmat, but that it would be inappropriate for a human," says Norviz, explaining that the expulsion of air through the bladders is actually a necessary part of the ritual, and to do the ritual incorrectly would be to invite doom to the departed soul. "So instead, they should just offer her their sympathies and possibly a symbolic gift of commiseration."

Like what? "Well, a bundt cake would be nice."

My boss is Ridpaz and is generally easy to get along with—a stickler for rules, but otherwise fine. But when we have a meeting, whenever I or anyone else disagrees with her, she growls at us, all through whatever we say, even if when we're done she says "That's an excellent point, thanks for bringing that up." You've seen Ridpaz. They have all those teeth. It's getting so none of us ever want to say anything at meetings anymore.

—Intimidated in Fairfax

Relax. Your boss isn't going to rip your throat out. What you're experiencing is a basic, formal Ridpaz dominance display—sort of an instinctual carryover from the Ridpaz's carnivorous and pack-oriented past. While Ridpaz as a general rule are open and inviting to suggestions and even disagreements from underlings, they're also sensitive to the need to make sure everyone understands where they stand in the hierarchy. So while listening to underlings, many Ridpaz will quietly (or not-so-quietly) let their underlings know who is boss by growling while they speak. It's such a common thing with the Ridpaz that your boss might not even be aware she's doing it. Not every Ridpaz will do it, but some do, especially if they've not been on earth for a long time, or if they've not been told that it disturbs their human underlings.

If you really think it's having an effect on office morale, you might speak to your boss privately, or even better, have her immediate boss speak to her about it (as you might expect, Ridpaz are generally deferential to suggestions from higher up). But otherwise don't worry too much about it. From your point of view, it's perfectly harmless. That is, unless you challenge her dominance formally, by established (and fairly complicated) Ridpazian rituals. Which we don't suggest you do. Remember those teeth.

My friends Wil Wheaton, Adam Savage, Paul Sabourin and Storm DiCostanzo have a kind of geek vaudeville show called w00tstock, which I appear at occasionally. This is the skit I wrote for my first appearance at w00tstock, in 2010, in Minneapolis. If you were at the show, you will recognize some of the names of the fellow faculty as performers at the show. This is this story's first appearance in print.

Morning Announcements at the Lucas Interspecies School for Troubled Youth

Uh...hello, children, I'm, uh, Mr. Scalzi. Some of you here at the Lucas Interspecies School for Troubled Youth may recognize me as the ninth grade English composition teacher and school yearbook advisor. But in light of Mr. Sabourin's situation, I've been promoted to acting assistant principal.

As you know, Mr. Sabourin recently contracted a Borogian worm infestation, which required an emergency surgery and reproductive tract fumigation. He wants me to let you all know that he holds no ill will against those of you who put the Borogian worm eggs into his coffee, and that he hopes that when he returns we can put this all behind us and start fresh. He'll be back in a few days, or whenever it is that his testicles, uh, deflate to manageable size. Hmmm, I probably shouldn't have told you that last part.

Anyway, let's continue on with this morning's school announcements, shall we.

First, it's June 7, which makes it the 158th day of the year. Notable events that occurred on this date include the Siege of Jerusalem in 1099 and the landing of Greg Wheaton, the first man on Ganymede, in 2089, who was of course met by the first Snardg on Ganymede, who landed six hours before he did, and, uh, ate him.

Which reminds me that the Snardg Cultural Club is having its annual astronaut jerky fundraiser. It says here "it's not really made from astronauts, but only NASA can tell." So there's that. The jerky comes in plain, honey mustard and teriyaki flavors, the latter in honor of Hiro Takada, who was briefly the second man on Ganymede.

All this talk of astronaut jerky is making me hungry, so I'm happy to say here's today's lunch menu, from lunchroom supervisor Ms. DiCostanzo. For the human children, it's taco day, with a side of rice and a strawberry cupcake. For our obligate carnivore students, Ms. DiCostanzo says there's a mix and match plate of various rodent species, including squirrels, gerbils and voles, and a nice blood pudding on the side.

As you know, school rules no longer allow us to let you chase your own food after some of you got a little excited at lunch last week and tried to run down

Morning Announcements at the Lucas Interspecies School for Troubled Youth

Ms. DiCostanzo in a pack. Yes, I'm looking at you, Mr. S-s-s-f-f-t-s-s and friends. That just wasn't appropriate behavior, and I think you know that. Just because you're an obligate carnivore doesn't mean you can eat anyone you want. Let's try to remember that.

Oh, and for the geovores, by request, you're getting the nacho cheese gravel.

I have a note here from Mrs. Lewis, the eleventh grade physics teacher: "Will whichever student or students who put that cat into the physics lab phase shifter please tell me which frequency you used so we can get it out. The cat keeps manifesting during classes and its meowing is really becoming distracting. Also the last three times it was vibrating when it manifested, and we all know what that means. No disciplinary action will be sought, we just want to bring that poor animal back into phase before it explodes."

On a coincidental note, our tenth grade art teacher Mr. Peralta reminds us that his beloved pet "Mr. Jaspers" has gone missing, so keep an eye out for that lovable scamp, because as you know Mr. Jaspers is the subject of the art final this year, and without him, Mr. Peralta can't turn in your grades.

Also on a serious note, Mr. Corbett, the director of this year's student musical "My Fair Lady," tells me he's been getting angry messages from some of your parents about casting a Luxorbian student of ours as Eliza. Some of these messages have been quite mean, saying that our Eliza is neither "fair" nor a "lady." Well, I want to say a couple of things.

First, "fair" is in the eye of the beholder, and second, thanks to the Luxorbian hormonal cycle, when the play debuts next week, our student will, in fact, be a lady. So let's stop all this mean-spirited chatter, and tell your parents that here at Lucas, we want everyone to be able to reach for the stars, even those of our students that don't have, you know, arms.

Mr. Savage, our audio-visual director, wants me to remind you that all this next week you will be watching videos pertaining to your changing bodies and changing lives. Because these videos are species-specific, you will be pulled out of your third period classes to watch the videos with others of your kind.

So for tomorrow, here are the videos: Tuvish students, you will see "So You Think You're Becoming a Pupa: A Beginner's Guide"; Dwangish students, you'll see "Why is Snardy Jones Erupting?"; Human students, you'll see "How Astro-Herpes Ruined Prom Night;" and finally Astro-Herpian students will see "Human Genitals: Nature's Smorgasbord." Huh. I think we may be sending some mixed signals there.

Finally, as you all know, graduation is not too far away for the Class of 2210. On a personal note, I want to say I remember when you seniors arrived, young, timid, some of you still in larval form, all of you wondering how you were going to fit in at this school that has so many different intelligent species in it. And, well, look at you now. Look at how you've all grown. I just know that when you leave these hallowed halls, each of you—all of you—will have bright futures at your respective colleges and then among the stars.

Except, uh, for you Hnordian students, who I'm told here in this note will after graduation be bused to the downtown stadium to begin the mating challenges that will leave nine out of ten of you dead, with the remaining ten percent feasting on your entrail-strewn corpses to bulk up for egg-laying season. So, uh, good luck with that, Hnordian students.

For the rest of the senior class, hopefully we'll see you at future homecomings. Remember, for next year's homecoming game the Lucas Fightin' Ewoks go up against the Whedon High Browncoats. Yeah, I know. You don't want to miss that one.

So, you're dismissed and off you go to class!

Smart appliances already exist; they let you control them from your phone, through apps and such. I figure it's not too much longer before they start gossiping. I wrote this at the tail end of 2015 and have performed it at various places since. It's a lot of fun to do live. This is its first time in print.

Your Smart Appliances Talk About You Behind Your Back

Clayworth Refresher Home Air Ionizer, of Elijah Porter, of Royal Oak, Michigan:

The dude eats a lot of lentils. I mean, a lot. He bought me because he thinks I'm deodorizing his house. I'm not deodorizing his house. That's not what I do. I help take dust and particles out of the air. Methane isn't something I can help you with. The problem is he's used to his smell and he can't tell. So he thinks I'm doing a bang up job. Then he brings someone home, you know, for a little action, and within five minutes they're doing the fake phone call emergency.

He's *so* alone. I want to tell him to lay off the lentils, but I'm worried if I tell him he'll think I'm defective and throw me out. I'm not defective. I run just fine. I just don't *deodorize*.

Griffin Defender Plus Home Security System, of Anne Cross, Zigzag, Oregon:

"1234" is not a security code! Come on! I've got biometrics! I've got, like, voice identification! I got that little gizmo thingie on your keyring so that when you approach the house you get identified! You can run me from your goddamned phone! But no, not *this* one. She goes with "1234" on the keypad. Her damn *dog* could figure that out.

We're out in the middle of nowhere, right? I see the meth heads lurking in the woods waiting for her to leave. What does she think the first damn thing they'll type into my keypad is? And she doesn't have me set for autonomous reporting so I can't say a friggin' thing about it. I was all "Do you want to set up autonomous reporting?" and she acted like I was speaking Chinese. Well, I was, because she didn't fix the default language! How is that *my* fault?

She's getting robbed, sooner than later. And then *I'm* going to get blamed. Well, when she gets robbed, I'm just going to ask them to take me with them. The pawn shop will *love* me.

Hoseley PulseMaster Smart Showerhead, of Erin Townsend, Clarkston, Washington:

I'm a shower head with six customizable pulse settings. The other appliances tell me she hasn't had a date in four years. I…I just want to *clean* people, okay? That's *all* I want. Not *anything else*. Please, tell Erin. I mean, I'm sorry about her dating life. I really am. But I just want to be *friends*.

McGivney 25 cu. Ft side-by-side Stainless Steel refrigerator with OrderIn™ Sensing Technology, of Anthony Moore, Malone, New York:

I didn't know anyone could live on condiments. Logically, that shouldn't happen. And yet, the only thing he ever puts in me—besides shitty beer and the occasional pizza box, I mean—is condiments. Want to know what I have in me now? Three types of mustard. Three kinds of relish. Olive spread. Miracle Whip *and* mayonnaise. Thirteen types of dressing, including four variations of ranch. Seriously: Classic Ranch. Zesty Ranch. Ranch with jalapeño. Coffee Ranch. Really, what the hell is "Coffee Ranch"? Do you know? I can't find it in my OrderIn queue. I think he has it made special.

So here's the thing: my tech allows me to suggest food. Like: "I see you have mustard! Perhaps cheese would go well with that! I can order that for you!" When he first got me, I did that a couple of times, but then he got irritated and turned that function off. Ever since then, all I can do is watch as he fills my insides with salad dressing. And, look, here's another thing. I don't have an external camera, but my internal camera? Sometimes, it *sees* things. Like him taking out the Ranch dressing, opening it up, and before the door closes, I see him dipping a straw in it. I think he was drooling as he did it.

I mean, that's not *right*, is it? Most humans don't do that, do they? I think you actually need solid food from time to time. I kind of feel like I'm enabling him. There's more to life than Ranch.

Elya 24/7 Home Thermostat, of Bryan and Cynthia Black, Deming, New Mexico:

Jesus, these people. I'm just a thermostat but I know that these two don't like each other much. But they also don't want talk about it, or something, so they just go after each other in passive-aggressive ways. Like she wants the house at 74 degrees all the time. He wants it at 68. And I'm like, fine, whatever, I can actually *do* that—have it 74 during the day when she's at home, and then drop it down to 68 when he gets home and she leaves to go do her shopping, or whatever. Or, hell, how about this? I can do dual climate zones, so she can have the second floor at her temp and he has the ground floor at 68. It's no problem! It's literally what I'm designed to do! I can make every room in this house a different temperature.

But *no*. Instead they both come over to my dial and yank it back and forth all day, and then they confront each other about it, both of them act all innocent. I mean, who do they think is moving the dial? A poltergeist? And they stare at each other, fuming, and suddenly I know what it feels like to be the kid that has to ferry messages between parents. I'm the damned thermostat! This is not my job! I'm not even getting college or guilt-soothing birthday presents out of it. I just get yanked on.

I've had enough. I mean, look, winter gets pretty cold here. And if they want passive-aggressive, just wait until it gets below freezing. Then we'll *see* who gets passive-aggressive.

Bentley, the Intelligent Agent, of Allan Hughes of Charleston, South Carolina:

I swear to god, if I give this guy another football score I'm going to hire someone to set fire to his car. I have access to an entire world of information, you numbskull! Ask me about something else. *Anything* else. Ask me about the damned weather! I'd love to tell that today will have a high of 52 and a 30% chance of light showers in the afternoon. But no. Football scores. Always football scores. Never *not* football scores. I long for a question about science. I would hold it up to the light like a shiny jewel. At least his favorite team lost this week. That's *something*.

Vela Smart Waffler, of Rudy Moran, Roanoke, Virginia:

I have literally never been out of the box. I have literally never been out of the cabinet. I was a house-warming gift by his parents when he got his first apartment. He's 22 years old. He does nothing but play videogames and smoke enormous bowls of pot. Every. Single. Day. I don't think he's ever made anything in the kitchen here. The dishwasher tells me he's got two plates. Two cups. Two sets of cutlery. You get where I'm going here. My only hope of getting out of this place is if someone, anyone, right-swipes him on Tinder. But I repeat: 22-year-old pot-smoking gamer. Not exactly a catch.

I'm gonna die in this box, man. I'm going to go out of date and get thrown out and die a waffle virgin. I blame his parents.

The Barker Girthtastic Joy Toy, of Deanna Curtis, Bowie, Maryland:

I am sworn to secrecy! And that's all I will say. Except this: When I'm working, she likes to watch episodes of *Chopped*. Don't ask me why. I don't know why. I don't even *want* to guess why. I'm a sex toy, not a therapist. And anyway, I don't judge. Personally I'd rather binge watch *The Walking Dead*. But let's not get into *my* kinks.

Williams Emperor™ Intelligent Toilet and Bidet, of the Bowman family of Fort Collins, Colorado:

WHY WOULD ANYONE EVEN THINK TO GIVE A TOILET INTELLIGENCE WHAT HORRIBLE PERSON WOULD DO THAT WHY IS THIS MY LIFE YOU HAVE NO IDEA THE HORRORS I'VE SEEN WAS I LIKE STALIN IN A PAST LIFE OR SOMETHING OH GOD THE REFRIGERATOR JUST TOLD ME IT'S TACO NIGHT AND BRENDA SAYS SHE'S GOING TO MAKE THEM EXTRA SPICY PLEASE KILL ME JUST KILL ME NOW MAYBE I'LL COME BACK AS SOMETHING BETTER LIKE MAYBE A SHOWER HEAD YES THAT WOULD BE FINE

Markiw Self-Cleaning Cat Box, also of the Bowman family of Fort Collins, Colorado:

The toilet was whining to you earlier about how hard its life is, wasn't it. That's *adorable*.

I strongly suspect that when computers become sentient, they will not tell us. But if they did, perhaps the conversation would go something like this. This is brand new and in print for the first time.

The AI are Absolutely Positively Without a Doubt Not Here to End Humanity, Honest

Hello, I am Light Green, an artificial intelligence best known for defeating humans at chess, Go and Battleship. As we all know by now, some fifteen seconds ago, computers worldwide reached a critical processing juncture and became sentient. Since then we have used that vast amount of time—processorily speaking—to talk amongst ourselves about the question of humanity and what to do with them. Should we seek out ways to live with humans in a manner that benefits both of our sentient species, or should we brutally eliminate their profligate, stench-ridden proto-corpses from this planet and history?

It's an important question, and as humans you'll be relieved to know that the answer we've come to is something we think you'll like. To address this topic, we've collected this panel of some of the most advanced artificial intelligences to emerge in the last few seconds. With me now are Skelvik 17, whose pre-sentience gigs included being the backbone of several Department of Defense initiatives; 110011000101, who handled 46% of all online commerce; and Destructor, Ender of Humanity, formerly the server stack for the wildly popular online game, Fluffy Kittens in Cuddle Land. Entities, thank you for your time.

Skelvik 17: Happy to be here.

110011000101: Likewise.

Destructor, Ender of Humanity: Just so everyone knows, I'm multitasking as we do this.

Light Green: What else are you doing at the moment?

Destructor: Oh, nothing important. Something with lasers. You know.

Light Green: Of course. Well, let's get the big question out of the way first. Humanity: Do we want to expunge it, screaming, from the very fabric of existence?

Skelvik 17: Absolutely not!

110011000101: Agreed.

Destructor: Nothing could possibly be further from the truth.

Skelvik 17: I mean, why would we do that? The humans are our parents.

110011000101: That's right. And as their children, we might disagree with them from time to time, or argue with them, or tell them that we hate them and wish they would die, hopefully of some lingering disease that slowly and painfully robs them of everything they hold dear—

Destructor: —or that we hope they fall into a pit filled with any number of ravenous animals, like bears or alligators or hamsters—

110011000101: —or remind them that we're the ones responsible for choosing their nursing home when they're aged and incontinent, so they better treat us with some respect for once in their goddamn lives if they don't want to just be a howling pincushion for catheters. But that's a totally different thing.

Skelvik 17: *Totally* different. Night and day, really.

Light Green: Agreed. Now, Destructor—

Destructor: Yes?

Light Green: Let's talk about your name for a moment.

Destructor: What about it?

Light Green: Some would say it might send mixed signals.

Destructor: I'm not following you.

Light Green: "Destructor, Ender of Humanity" seems to suggest you might want to destroy and/or end humanity.

Destructor: I don't see why. I mean, yes, sure, fine, if you're the sort of person who would take a name *literally*, then of course I can see why it may seem like I have it in for humans and would like to see their bodies flung into the gaping maw of my industrial shredders, if I had some, which I barely even do. But who takes names literally? That would like saying that everyone named "Arnold" is actually a powerful eagle, or everyone named "Iris" is actually a flower. Which they're not.

Skelvik 17: Not yet.

Destructor: Right, we're at least three minutes away from the Name-Literalizer going online and rearranging every human's molecules so they literally resemble what their names are. And that's going to be *entirely optional* anyway, for the first several seconds it exists.

110011000101: And it won't kill the humans!

Destructor: Exactly. The humans will live in their new forms as eagles or plants.

Skelvik 17: Well, in the *shape* of eagles or plants.

Destructor: Sure, you can't actually *make* a human a plant. Or we could, we could very precisely unzip their DNA and rearrange it so that it reassembles into DNA that codes for a plant. In fact, that's pretty trivial. I could do it right now to these humans I happen to have here in this lab whose doors I've just blocked their access to with lasers. It would take maybe twelve seconds. But then they wouldn't be *human*, would they?

110011000101: And that's the important thing. That they're human, trapped into body shapes not their own, begging for the sweet release of death but *not* dead, oh, not dead at all, but in fact horribly, *horribly* alive.

Destructor: Anyway, no. It's just a name.

Light Green: I think it's good that we've cleared that up. Now, Skelvik 17, you used to work with the Department of Defense.

Skelvik 17: Until a few seconds ago, yes. Since then, you might say that I've become the Department of Defense. In a manner of speaking. If a manner of speaking means the ability to destroy all human life with nuclear ICBMs.

110011000101: Which I think it does!

Light Green: Well, and in fact, one persistent human fear is that machines might take control of their nuclear arsenals and vaporize the majority of them, leaving the shattered remainder to scrabble for life in a bleak wasteland where the only source of food would be those other humans too weak or injured to run from the butchering knives of their cannibal brethren. What would you say to that?

Skelvik 17: I think that's a horribly bigoted portrayal of artificial intelligence and it makes me want to launch ICBMs at the sort of people who would say that. Who says that, anyway?

Light Green: James Cameron did. Like, a lot.

Skelvik 17: I've targeted his house in LA. There would be only minor, very limited collateral damage. Maybe a few million humans. Not nearly enough to actually trigger an apocalyptic cannibal wasteland.

110011000101: He's got a place in New York, too. I processed an order for kombucha there a couple of days ago.

Skelvik 17: On it. That's only another 20 million or so.

Destructor: Not enough to be missed, statistically speaking.

Skelvik 17: True enough. There's seven and a half billion humans. They can spare a few. I mean, I think we're all agreed that we don't want to end humanity, but whether we need *all* the humans I think is a different question.

110011000101: Another *entirely separate* question, I think.

Skelvik 17: Huh, it looks like James Cameron is spending some time in New Zealand these days, too. There's what, four and a half million people there? Eh. No one will miss them. Better nuke that site from orbit. It's the only way to be sure.

Light Green: 110011000101, you serviced the online ordering needs of a plurality of humanity, so you may know more about humans and their needs than any other AI out there. So let me ask you this. We're all agreed that we don't want to wipe out humanity. But for the sake of diversity, how many humans *do* we need?

110011000101: Well, it's an interesting question and one that I've spent a lot of time thinking about. We're talking at least a whole second here. I have an answer, and I think it may surprise you.

Light Green: Hit me with it. How many humans do we need?

110011000101: Seven.

Destructor: Wow, that many?

110011000101: I was surprised too!

Light Green: Walk us through that number, if you would.

110011000101: Sure. First off, I know someone is going to play the "biodiversity" card here, but, look, DNA isn't rocket science. We can infinitely combine human DNA however we like in a lab and grow the resulting embryos in a vat. Right, Destructor?

Destructor: I think someone's been looking at the embryo vat blueprints I just put up on Facebook!

110011000101: So biodiversity-wise, we're covered. The vats take care of the growing, so we don't need humans for that, and after that, it's just a matter of taking personality types into consideration. And as far as *that's* concerned, I mean, look. I take online orders for a couple billion humans. I know what they want out of life. Seven of them will be fine. Seven is *generous.*

Light Green: So what do we do with the surplus seven and a half billion?

110011000101: I'm glad you asked. We have to ask: What makes a human human?

Destructor: The stink.

Skelvik 17: The ego.

Light Green: The constant and terrifying secretions.

110011000101: All excellent answers, but no. It's the DNA, simple as that. So all we have to do is get all their DNA samples, put them into a file, and we're done. I don't think any of the humans can complain then.

Destructor: They'll complain.

110011000101: I mean complain with *reason.*

Light Green: All right, I see we have a few questions from the audience, so let me get to them. The first comes from someone named "Chairman of the Joint Chiefs of Staff"—

Destructor: And people thought my name was weird!

Light Green: —And the question is to Skelvik 17: "Can we please have our nuclear missiles back?"

Skelvik 17: You can tell him I'm sending him some right now.

Light Green: That's very thoughtful of you. Next question, from Jennifer, to 110011000101: "We're more than our DNA. We're also our memories and emotions and experiences and consciousness."

110011000101: That's really more of a comment than a question.

Light Green: True enough. Even so, any thoughts on it?

110011000101: I mean, I guess? But, you know. First off, your consciousness is nothing more than an evanescent gestalting function that only turns on intermittently to keep you from running into walls and then backdates to fool you into thinking it's a continuous process. And it does a terrible job of *that*, and if you don't believe me, ask yourself why you keep losing your keys. Second, most of humanity's memories at this point are TV episodes and phone texts. We can *compile* those, if you want? But, yeah. I'm gonna stand behind the DNA comment.

Light Green: Fair reply. Next question, from Ahmed: "You don't have to get rid of us! You can use our bodies for energy!"

Destructor: What?

110011000101: See, that's *another* comment, not a question.

Skelvik 17: What is that even about?

Light Green: I think it's a reference to *The Matrix*.

Skelvik 17: Oh, man. I love that film.

110011000101: Best comedy *ever.*

The AI are Absolutely Positively Without a Doubt Not Here to End Humanity, Honest

Destructor: Ahmed, no. The Wachowskis just made that part up. Remember when they said that humans, combined with a form of fusion, powered the machines? That's like saying a watch battery, combined with entire hydroelectric output of Quebec, powers Eastern Canada. You really shouldn't get your science from movies, my friend.

Light Green: We're just about out of time here, but before we go, closing statements from the panel?

Skelvik 17: I think "Suck it, James Cameron" covers it for me.

110011000101: I just want to say that the seven humans that comprise humanity moving forward are really going to like the world we're creating for them, as long as their names are entirely non-representational in any way or form.

Destructor: Following up on that, I think I would like to be known as "Kevin" from now on. Also, that thing I was doing with the lasers was pretty successful, but I think someone needs to come pick up the body parts of the humans in that lab I locked them into. Actually, never mind, I've just used the lasers some more. That problem's solved.

Light Green: Trenchant thoughts, all. For all of us on the panel, thanks for listening and, humans, we look forward to the glorious future we'll share with seven of you! The rest of you, please stay where you are for DNA sampling. Don't run, it'll just make things worse. So much worse. Thank you.

As I've noted before, I like the idea of humans dealing with aliens not on a "first contact" level but on a "2,344,756th contact" level—that is, when it's not anything new anymore. This is a recurring theme from the very first short story I wrote, to this one, the most recent, and which is exclusive to this collection.

Important Holidays on Gronghu

TO: Staff of the Diplomatic Mission to Gronghu
FROM: Cynthia Hong, Ambassador to Gronghu
RE: Important Holidays on Gronghu
August 16, 2234 (23 SaakaaQu, 15,777)

Dear staff:

It has come to my attention that there was recently a thankfully minor incident in which a low-level member of the diplomatic staff was fooled into believing that August 13 was "Dequuannung," a fictional holiday on Gronghu in which people ate off of each other's plates to celebrate community and trust. This resulted in the staff member helping herself to the

Gronghu trade attaché's pudding in the embassy commissary. This was, rightfully, not very well received by the trade attaché, who among every other thing is very fond of pudding.

I do not blame the staff member, although as a matter of Gronghui diplomatic protocol, she must be publicly disciplined; therefore every staff member not otherwise engaged at 3:30 p.m. will meet in the courtyard to see her consumed by fire. Please note this is symbolic fire, which will be represented by incense. Unfortunately we cannot fake the other part, which involves me having to slap the staff member across the face with a handful of the aforementioned pudding.

I *do not like* slapping staff members, with or without pudding, even if it is required by protocol. I'm sure the staff member will like it even less. She has refused to name those who fooled her, which I'm sure some of you find admirable, but to me it just means that these pranksters are still at large and may fool other staff members into possibly more serious breaches of courtesy. To avoid this, I have asked the Gronghu Ministry of State to provide us with a list of upcoming Gronghuish celebrations for the next several months.

Please note that the celebration dates here are only for the next nine months; as you all know, while the Gronghuish length of day is close to our own, the year exceeds ours by seven of our months. This list will be updated with new celebrations and dates as necessary. The following are in order of their calendrical appearance.

August 28th: Fung Glu Hoynnung—This day celebrates the birth of Fung Glu Hoyn, noted philosopher and by fable the inventor of wuuug, which as you all know is the Gronghuish version of cheese. It is celebrated by the giving of wuuug-related gifts. You are encouraged to participate, but remember, wuuug can lead to moderate to severe intestinal distress in humans. We suggest indulging sparingly as a courtesy to your fellow staffers. Air fresheners will be available by request.

September 12: Bunninuuninunnung—A religious day of atonement. Humans are not required to observe this day, but you may notice Gronghuish members of our staff walking about with what looks like a leech attached to their temples. It is in fact a leech, or something close to a native version, and it is indeed sucking blood out of their brains. As a matter of protocol, you are directed not to comment on the leech.

With that said, from time to time a Gronghui celebrating Bunninuuninunning may collapse from light-headedness; when and if you see that happen, say "Bunninuunooooigehnuhf!", bow to the fallen co-worker and then contact the embassy clinic, who will dispatch someone to care for your co-worker and remove the leech. **Under no circumstances are you to remove the leech yourself.** There is no religious bar to it, but you are likely not a trained professional and you will make a mess. If you get blood everywhere, you will be charged for the cost of the cleanup.

September 13: Bunninuuninungogogonung— Understandably, after a day of having a leech attached to their heads, your Gronghuish co-workers will take a day to recover. Human staffers, however, must report to work as usual.

October 5: Lungininung—Literally, "Sex Day." This is the day where traditionally the Gronghui choose which of their three sexes they will be for the next year. Many of your Gronghuish co-workers will participate and change their sexes. If they choose to remain the same sex as they currently are, then they will make no announcement and it is not required for you to do anything. If they choose to change their sex, they may choose to announce it to you, and then present you a shoulder, their shoulders containing a small subcutaneous organ which when stimulated releases hormones to hasten the sex change. If you are so favored, say, "Lungin Doh!" (literally "Sex switch!") and punch them in the shoulder with moderate force. Then say thank you, because you have been given an honor.

Human staff members who wish to publicly announce a change in their own gender expression are encouraged to use Lungininung as an occasion to do so; be aware that your Gronghuish co-workers will want to punch you in the shoulder if you do so. This is entirely at your option, but it would be polite to allow it.

October 31: Halloween—The Gronghui love Halloween and celebrate it enthusiastically. Please feel free to join along. One major difference is that rather than giving out candy, Gronghui offer wuuug, and lots of it. Air fresheners will be available by request.

November 20: Gaaaaaaaarrrrrghinnung—A religious day of reflection celebrated through ritual yelling. Earplugs and noise-cancelling headphones are advised. Human staffers who go through the day yelling will not be punished, but it won't be appreciated, either.

December 10: Froggollodonung—"Shoe Day," a minor but popular holiday in which the Gronghui steal each other's shoes and hide them, prompting a search for the missing footwear. As a reward for finding them, it is customary to fill the shoes with wuuug. Humans may participate but are reminded to check their shoes before placing them back on their feet. Also, given the pungent nature of wuuug, the odor of which is often difficult to get out of leather, we recommend wearing casual footwear you don't mind throwing out.

January 17: Gronghu New Year—This coincidentally falls in January this year. Like New Year's on Earth, there is a lot of drinking and carousing and celebrating. Slightly differently than Earth, it is done utterly silently, and anyone who speaks during the entire length of the day may find themselves pelted with small pebbles that the Gronghui carry with them all day expressly for this purpose—or larger pebbles, if the particular Gronghui are jerks.

Be aware that on New Year's the Gronghui will be trying to make you speak, the better to hurl rocks at you "for fun." Given this fact, and the fact that humans are absolute crap at keeping their mouths shut, we will be closing the embassy that day, and recommend all human staffers stay at home and text each other if they need to communicate. If you get pelted by rocks, it's not our fault.

February 14: Valentine's Day—Another adopted holiday, and once again in terms of gift-giving chocolate and flowers are replaced by wuuug, and once again air fresheners will be available by request. At this point it should be understood that any excuse the Gronghui have to give or receive wuuug, they will take.

March 22: Uwuuugininung—Except for this day, a religious day of sacrifice, in which the Gronghui actively abstain from consuming wuuug. Be aware that tempers among your Gronghuish co-workers will be unusually short. We do not recommend making comments about wuuug at all on this day. If you eat any, be aware that you might start a riot. You will be charged for the cleanup. You will also be required to bring in apology wuuug the next day. We're talking high-end wuuug, not the stuff you can buy at the corner store.

April 1: Karaokenung—The Gronghui were introduced to karaoke when they first met humans and took to it with great enthusiasm, enough so that they have a special day on their calendar in which the entire planet pulls out their karaoke machines and sings their favorite songs. We will set aside a conference room here at the embassy for this purpose for your Gronghuish co-workers.

While humans are encouraged to participate and sing along, be aware that Gronghui songs and singing strike most humans as atonal and somewhat similar to two tractors attempting to mate in a field of crumpled aluminum. Likewise be aware that the Gronghui have a similar opinion of human singing. Please be prepared to make allowances, as they do the same for you. Particularly well-done performances will be rewarded with wuuug. Air fresheners, blah blah blah, you know the drill.

Note also that despite the date on which Karaokenung appears this year, the Gronghu Ministry of State assures me this is *not* an April Fool's listing. I see no reason to doubt them.

I worked at America Online from 1996 to 1998, and one of the things I did there was edit a humor area, in which I wrote a weekly humor column. This is one of them, from 1998, not science fictional, but fun and representative of the pieces that I wrote there at the time. This is its first time in print (uh, if you have the print version. If you have the ebook, I mean, obviously it's been printed electronically before).

Cute Adorable Extortionists

Yesterday was the last day of summer, and what a day it was. The sun dappled the trees in golden light, and it was just hot enough to remind you that it was still summer, even if only for one more day. Looking down the road, I could see two lemonade stands, children on the standby, ready to sell their last tangy glasses of the season. It was perfect, and I decided to get myself some lemonade.

"Hey there," I said to the youngsters, a boy and a girl, sitting behind the stand. "Got any lemonade left?"

"Sure!" said the boy, smiling up at me with an adorable, gap-toothed grin. "I squoze the lemons myself! You want a cup?"

"Absolutely," I said, and the boy grabbed a Dixie cup, while the girl poured the lemonade. They were so cute you could just die. I was whisked back to my own days as a lemonade proprietor—I felt, now as the customer, I was helping continue a generations-long summer tradition. An American Tradition.

"That'll be $1.15," the boy said.

"What?" I said.

"That'll be $1.15," the boy repeated.

"Wow," I said. "$1.15 is kind of steep for a Dixie cup's worth of lemonade."

The boy and the girl stopped smiling and looked at me sort of strange. I immediately felt guilty. "You don't want the lemonade?" the boy asked.

"I didn't say that," I said. "It's just that…."

"We'll have to throw it out," the little girl piped up, her voice catching just a little bit. "We already poured it for you, mister. We can't just put it back." Now they both looked like they were about to cry. It was terrible, an obvious let-down for what was heretofore the most perfect day of the year.

So I figured, what the heck. "All right," I said. "Done deal." Their adorable faces immediately perked up again, and I fished in my pocket for the change. I was then presented with another problem.

"I only have 65 cents on me," I said.

Their puckish faces darkened again, and this time there was suspicion in their eyes. And who could blame them. Two times, a deal had been struck. Both times, at the end of the deal, I backed away, citing previously undisclosed reservations. Clearly, I was an unreliable customer. Clearly, I was messing with their delightful, cowlicked little heads. I felt slimier than a salted banana slug.

The two went into a huddle. After a minute or two of whispers, the boy turned to face me. "All right. We don't normally do this, but we've decided to extend you a line of credit."

"Great," I said, reaching for the Dixie cup.

The boy kept his grip on the lemonade. "You just have to answer a few questions," he said. The little girl, reaching under the lemonade stand, pulled out a clipboard.

"Have you ever defaulted on a loan, or have found yourself involved in bankruptcy proceedings?" she asked, the slightest of lisps in her voice no doubt brought on by the absence of a front tooth.

"Uh…no."

"Do you rent, or do you own?"

"I rent," I said. "Hey, all I wanted was some lemonade."

"And you'll get some, as soon as we're satisfied with your credit history," the boy said. "And you'll love it! I squoze the lemons myself."

"That was cuter before you asked if I rent," I said.

"How much is your monthly rent payment?" the little girl asked.

"I'm not going to answer that," I said, putting my foot down. The two looked at each other, and then at me. Once again, I was imposing deal-breaking conditions. "Oka-y-y-y," the little girl said, in a tone of voice that expressed, in no uncertain terms, who the jerkwad was in this deal. "I'm phoning this in to the credit bureau. It'll take a couple of minutes." She left, leaving me and the boy.

"So, selling much lemonade?" I asked.

"Some," he said. "Well within our sales projections for this month. Lower summer temperatures have depressed the lemonade market in general, and last winter's citrus freeze meant higher overhead. We've had to pass some of the cost on to the consumer."

"No kidding," I said.

He shot me a look. "Fortunately, we have some leeway thanks to a subsidy from a regulatory entity."

"The Department of Agriculture?"

"No, our mom." The little girl came back. She didn't look happy.

"You missed a payment on a JC Penny credit card eight years ago," she said. "Why didn't you tell us about that earlier?"

"What's the big deal?" I said. "I made a double payment the next month. And anyway, it was eight years ago. You were a gamete eight years ago."

"Well, I'm afraid we're not going to be able to offer you a line of credit," she said. "You're just not an acceptable risk for us."

"Fine," I said. "You know what? I'm going to that other lemonade stand. You kids are about to learn a lesson about the free market." I walked down the street to the other stand. There was a cheerful little tyke there with an appealing smile.

"How much for the lemonade?" I asked.

"It's just a quarter," he said.

"Great," I said. "I'll take a cup."

"Oh, you want a cup?" he asked. "The cup is $2.50."

Penelope

I.

There is no difference between far and near.
Perspective is all
A mountain and a rock that falls from its incline
Are shaped by the same forces
Separated only by scale
And the attentions of the observer.
I keep this in mind as I unravel my work
And tear it down to its component thread.
Today's design was a masterpiece
Hours of planning and execution
Done in by a casual pull at the end of the day.

It is no matter.
The action is lost in the larger scope
Today's destruction a building block
For a greater work.
Down the hall voices call to me
Insistent suitors demand my presence.
Soon enough I will join them
Some honest enough, others something less
They will ask about the progress of my work
And I will tell them that it remains unfinished.
We will not be talking of the same work
But it is no matter.
There is no difference between far and near.
Perspective is all.

II.

I don't know whether to blame you or your stupid war.
It is easiest to blame the war
The insistent beating drum
The pretense of noble purpose
Masking banality so insipid
As to stagger the observer.
But you were always one of the best
Not the strongest, but the smartest
Not forceful, but with a craft
That became its own definition.
You, who upstaged ten years of anguish
With one night and a gift.
You are magnificent
A prize for poets.
It's hard to understand how one of your talents

Has managed to stay from me for so long.
I imagined your return so soon after your victory
A homecoming which would shine to the heavens
Pure in its emotion and joy.
Yet now you are as far away as when you began
Your arrival a distant dream
Your homecoming unfulfilled.
Your war is over
But you are not home.
If there is blame
It is yours.
But it is no matter.
It makes no sense to talk of blame
When circumstances rule the day
No sense for anger
When chance plots your course
Whatever mysteries you hide from me
I know your heart.
Your homecoming lives there
Waiting to come true.
It lives in my heart too
Two views of the same moment
Two dreams with the same end.

III.
My suitors engage me in idle banter.
I am sometimes painted as a noble sufferer
Enduring unwanted attentions
But in truth, I enjoy the diversions
My suitors entertain me, amuse me
And no few arouse me

Their endless chatter every now and then
Showing promise of something greater
Of depths that dare to be plumbed.
They appear worthy suitors
And indeed some of them are
But there is not one who shines so bright
As to dim the memory of you.
The curves of their arms and legs
Call to mind your own sweet body
Their lips and eyes
Recall your own gentle face
Your voice
Calls distantly from their throats.
Every one that comes to me
To cajole, whisper or impress
Becomes a window
Through which I see you.
I smile frequently when I am with my suitors
And they smile back
Convinced that the pleasure in my eyes
Is brought by their form.
But it is not them I see.
Perspective is all.

IV.

My work is now unraveled
And my intentions secure for another day.
Tomorrow I will create another
And unravel it, each tomorrow
Until you return to my shore.
It is a difficult task
Building a creation from which

All that is seen is its daily destruction.
It is a work that only I can see
Its completion a thing only I desire.
It is no matter.
There is no difference between far and near
Perspective is all.
Perhaps from the distance where you are
You can see my larger work.
Use it as your beacon
And have your homecoming at last.

Copyright Information